"NO! DON'T DO IT!"

"Ma!" I held her arm. "I have something I want to tell you. I'm calling the Wellses. Everyone in the phone book with the same last name as us."

"Why?"

"Maybe one of them is related to my father."

"I'll tell you right now. No! I don't want you to do this, Jessie."

"What if one of those people knows where James Wells is?"

"Jess, don't do it. There're a lot of things you don't know. Nothing will come of it but grief."

She put her hands around my face and looked at me steadily. "I love you, sweetie. Could you just take my word and not do it?"

Other Avon Flare Books by
Norma Fox Mazer

AFTER THE RAIN
BABYFACE
DOWNTOWN
MRS. FISH, APE, AND ME, THE DUMP QUEEN
OUT OF CONTROL
SILVER
TAKING TERRI MUELLER

NORMA FOX MAZER

Missing Pieces

AN AVON FLARE BOOK

AVON BOOKS
A division of
The Hearst Corporation
1350 Avenue of the Americas
New York, New York 10019

Copyright © 1995 by Norma Fox Mazer
Published by arrangement with the author
Library of Congress Catalog Card Number: 94-39271
ISBN: 0-380-72289-5
RL: 5.8

Published in hardcover by William Morrow and Company, Inc.; for information address Permissions Department, William Morrow and Company, Inc.,
1350 Avenue of the Americas, New York, New York 10019.

First Avon Flare Printing: September 1996

AVON FLARE TRADEMARK REG. U.S. PAT. OFF. AND IN OTHER COUNTRIES,
MARCA REGISTRADA, HECHO EN U.S.A.

Printed in the U.S.A.

RA   10 9 8 7 6 5 4 3 2 1

Contents

The Disappearing Dude

When I was small, my mother always began my favorite story by saying, "This is the story of my life, Jessie. It starts when I was a little girl, just like you."

Sitting on her lap and staring up into her face, I was amazed to think that my big, soft mommy had once been a child, too.

"I had a mother and a father," my mother continued, "and everything was nice until I was nine years old. My father went fishing on a big lake, Oneida Lake, and a storm came up, and the wind blew and there were big waves."

"How big?" I asked.

"Big, Jessie! Big! My father didn't know how to swim, and he wasn't wearing a life jacket. The boat went over and he drowned. Jeez!"

She always said *jeez* like that when she got upset. I petted her cheek and said I would never get drowned and make her sad. She hugged me close, and I snuggled in, because now the story got even sadder.

"My mother got married again," she went on, "and you know, her husband was my stepfather, right? Well, he didn't like me. Every day it was, 'Maribeth, you make too much noise. Maribeth, shut your big mouth. Maribeth, you are a brat.' "

"But your mama loved you," I said.

"Yes, she did."

"Just like you love me."

"Then my mother got cancer and died. Now, don't cry," she said quickly. "Are you going to cry?"

I shook my head hard. "You won't die, will you, Mama?"

"Not for a long, long time, sweetie. Not till I'm an old bent lady with no teeth." She showed me her teeth. "See how strong they are?"

"Will Aunt Zis die? Her teeth aren't so strong."

"She won't die for a long, long time, either."

"Promise?" I would sit there, my four-year-old heart beating fast, waiting to hear her promise, as if her words alone could keep her and Aunt Zis safe.

"Want me to stop, Jessie? Are you getting too upset, baby?"

"No! Keep telling." It was a thrilling story, scarier, sadder, and much better than any of the stories Aunt Zis read me at night, which were usually about bunnies and bears.

"After my mother died, my stepfather told me he was going to move to Denver. He had a son there, from when he was married before. He didn't want to take me with him. He didn't exactly say that, but he told me he didn't know how he got stuck with a fourteen-year-old girl."

The part about Denver and the son was a little confusing, but I knew what came next. "You said, 'I don't want to go with you.' And he said, 'Well, hell, that's fine with me, but you better find somebody to live with.' "

"You got it. I didn't know what I was going to do. Who could I live with? I didn't have anyone. Then—"

"I know! I know!" I sat up, excited. "Just like in a

fairy tale, you remembered that your mama had an aunt!''

"And she lived in New York City. But how was I going to find her? New York City! One of the biggest cities in the whole world. Millions of people, Jessie. It was a miracle I found her. And you know what she did?''

"What?'' I knew, but I wanted to hear my mother say it.

"She got right on the train and came up here. Day one, I talked to her. Day two, she was here. Day three, she said to my stepfather, 'Go! We don't need you.' She rescued me. She saved my life. She didn't have to do that, did she? She could have said, 'Sorry. I'm not a young woman. No fourteen-year-old girls for me, either.' ''

"But she didn't say it!'' I quickly kissed my mother.

"And you know something else she could have said? 'Maribeth, you come live with me in New York City.' ''

"Anybody else would have said that.'' I said it before my mother could, and I got another hug for remembering.

"Aunt Zis said I didn't need to change schools and cities and friends, besides everything else. She said I'd had enough stuff in my life, we would just live right here.''

"And so you did! Now tell me the James Wells part.''

My mother took a breath. "I was seventeen, and one day I met this guy in a record store and—''

"This guy in a record store who had a big voice, like me,'' I reminded her.

"Right.''

"And beautiful eyebrows, like me.''

"What else?''

"Strong as a little horse.''

She nodded. "He worked in lots of countries, on high-

3

ways and bridges. He worked in Canada, Brazil, Saudi Arabia. He had two leather jackets and a BMW. He once paid fifty dollars for a silk tie. When he got dressed up, he looked like a prince!"

"And then you got married to the prince, even though Aunt Zis didn't want you to, so young, and you were beautiful."

"Uh-huh. And then he wanted to buy a house, one of those brick ones with three fireplaces and three garages and three *bathrooms*. Don't I wish! But I found *this* little old house, which is so great, and all we could afford, anyway."

"Our house," I said with satisfaction. "And you moved in, and I was born, and I was wonderful."

"One hundred percent right on the mark! And then one day—"

I couldn't wait for her to say it. "James Wells said, 'I'm going out for a while.' "

"Uh-huh. And I said, 'Where are you going?' And he looked at his watch and said—"

" 'Nowhere special, be back in a few hours.' " This always hit my funny bone. "Nowhere special, be back in a few hours! But he never came back and you cried for three days!"

One day I added, "Because he was James Wells, the disappearing dude."

"Where'd you get that, you cutie? Zis," my mother called to my aunt, "did you hear what this child just said?" She couldn't stop laughing, and the disappearing dude became part of the story, too.

For years, my mother told me that story. For years, I loved it, and I listened, crying and laughing at all the right moments. Well, I was small. I was a child. Not that I'm an adult now, but I am fourteen, and it's different. I don't ask for the story anymore, and if my mother does refer to it, I hear it differently. It seems to me there's

4

something left out—it's like a frame without a picture. The frame is intricate, carved, full of detail, but in the center is an emptiness. Something is missing: James Wells. Who he was, what he was like, why he left us. Why he left me.

❁

The Tiniest Punctuation Mark in the World

I was in the attic, looking around, thinking I might find an old blouse of my mother's that would be fun to wear to school. I sorted through boxes, opened and closed drawers, sneezing from the dust. I was ready to leave when I saw an edge of something metallic poking out of the back of a bureau drawer. I pulled at it, but it was jammed in tight. I got the pliers from the toolbox and pulled out a brass buckle engraved with the letters JW. I thought, Jessie Wells. Then I knew. JW. James Wells. I was astonished to be holding something that had belonged to him.

I went downstairs and polished the buckle and thought about James Wells choosing it, having the initials engraved, paying for it, taking it home. I imagined him fastening it to his belt, looking at himself in the mirror. I tried to see the expression on his face, but the fact was I didn't know what he looked like. *Strong as a little horse.* High cheekbones, I decided, and . . . long hair. He'd wear a big hat, a string tie, jeans. Was that James Wells? Why not? He could be anything I wanted him to be. He could be smart or dumb. A hero or a bum. The pliers had scratched the buckle—would he be angry if he knew, or would he laugh it off?

I dropped the buckle into the pocket of my winter jacket, let it drop out of my mind. But I started noticing disappearance stories again. The summer I was ten, I'd kept a scrapbook of them. Not just people—cars, cats, and dogs qualified, too. I remember one story that impressed me. CAT DISAPPEARS FROM HOME, REAPPEARS ONE YEAR LATER IN TREE. At the time I thought maybe the cat had been in the tree the whole year, which, in cat time, would have been seven years. I'd imagined him watching for seven cat years as his humans searched for him. Cat sense of humor. Or maybe he did get lost, and it took him seven cat years to find his way home. Cat persistence. I liked that even better.

People were always disappearing. Falling out of the world. You could say my family had a talent for it. Sometimes, like James Wells, they dropped out of sight with a lie and a smile and no reasons. Sometimes they disappeared and only the reasons remained, like ribbons or flags in the wind. My mother's father drowning because he was careless and didn't wear a life jacket. My mother's mother dying because, well, because she had bad luck.

Most of the people I read about in the newspapers, though, hadn't drowned or died. They'd done a James Wells thing, spiraling out of the world like a bit of smoke that leaves no trace. Gone in cars, trains, planes, buses. Gone on foot. Blurred figures moving, always moving away, becoming smaller and finer, whittled down by distance, until at last, at the horizon, where sky met land, nothing remained but a black dot, the tiniest punctuation mark in the world.

✷

THREE

Worlds and Anti-Worlds

Picture this: Open House at my school, and my mother, in her baggy-bottom gray pants that she fills out too well and her pilly blue sweater with the cigarette burn holes, zooming in on Meadow Cowan's mother, who is tall and thin like all the Cowans and is wearing something white and silky with big chunks of silver jewelry. It's like watching a broad-beamed barge bearing down on a sleek sailboat. Half of me wants to yell "Watch out!" to Mrs. Cowan, and the other half of me wants to grab my mom and hug her and hold her, just keep her from making a fool of herself.

I stood there for a while, and when I couldn't take another moment of watching her holding her elbows and talking, endlessly talking and blowing her nicotine breath into Mrs. Cowan's face, I walked away looking for Meadow.

In the front hall near the display case, I saw Aunt Zis and Mr. Novak, my social studies teacher. I never thought of Mr. Novak as especially big, but he loomed over her. Aunt Zis has always been small, but in the past few years she's gotten even tinier. She's shrinking. She looked great, dressed up as if she were going to work in a fancy office. Actually, she stopped working five years ago, when she was, as Ma says, "*only* seventy-eight."

I went to give her a little squeeze on the arm, but she sidestepped me. She's funny about what she calls "public displays of affection." She doesn't approve. At home she hugs and kisses me all the time, but as soon as we walk out the door, nothing doing.

I finally found Meadow in the gym, with her father, watching a gymnastics exhibition. "Jessie," she said, and she rose on her toes, as if being with her father made her so happy she was ready to float off into space.

"Hi, Med," I said. "Hello, Dr. Cowan." He's a dermatologist.

He peered at me as if I'd just arrived from a distant place. "Hello . . . er." I've seen that look before. Not a disagreeable one, only puzzled, as if he can't quite place me. He's absentminded. Also very fit—tall, lean, and blond, just like Meadow. They're both runners, too. They run together every morning.

Once, after her father had given me one of those hello . . . er looks, I made a joke about it to Meadow. I should have known better. She flew up in my face. "He's got a lot on his mind, Jessie! He's busy saving people's lives!"

"Silly me. I thought it was their complexions." I couldn't resist another joke.

Meadow started listing all the wonderful things her father had done: curing a man of a violent skin rash that was ruining his life; discovering that another patient was allergic to a whole spectrum of chemical substances. "That person couldn't even get up to make her kids breakfast, she was so sick. Until my father helped her."

"I know. I know. He's wonderful," I agreed. And smiled.

If I remember—and I usually do—I always agree and I always smile when Meadow and Diane, my other best friend, talk adoringly about their fathers. After all, they're the experts. And now, leaning against the wall, half-watching Lydia Sturmer walking delicately along the balance beam, I smiled again seeing Meadow possessively hold her father's arm and rise, rise on her toes.

Later, on the way home, I was thinking about Dr. Cowan's "Hello . . . er" greeting. He's known me as long as I've known Meadow, which is more than half my life, and yet he looked at me like a creature from another planet. *Well, yes, he's probably right. I am a creature from another planet. The Planet of No Fathers.*

"Ma." I leaned over the front seat. "I could not believe the way you were bending Mrs. Cowan's ear."

"What year?" Aunt Zis asked. She was sitting up front next to Ma. Her hearing is going a little.

"Ear, Aunt Zis, not year. Maribeth kept Meadow's mother standing there for an hour, yakking in her ear."

"Oh, I did not," my mother said. "An hour? Get out! Maybe ten minutes."

"No ten minutes, Ma! You were long-winded. You went on and on."

"Yeah, I love to talk. And so do you. We're just alike. My mother was like that, too. Loved to talk. She could talk your ear off about anything."

"Where did you get that idea, Maribeth?" Aunt Zis broke in. "She was a thinker. Like me. Like Jessie. Jessie resembles me a great deal."

I sat back while they argued over who I was most like. I do love to talk, but I like thinking, too, letting my mind roam away on ideas. *The father is driving the family home. . . . Next to him is his daughter. In the backseat, the mother and the aunt argue over who she takes after. The father glances at the daughter, winks. His wink says,* We *know who you take after. . . .*

Mrs. Scher, my English teacher, gave me a poem to read by a famous Russian poet. "I heard this man in a poetry reading once," she said. "Fabulous, Jessie. Beautiful words, plus ideas. I think you're going to be intrigued by this.'' The poem was called ''Worlds and Anti-Worlds,'' and the idea was that for everything we know of this world—for every action, every sequence of events, every moment—its opposite exists somewhere. Worlds and anti-worlds.

Imagine that James Wells hadn't walked out that cold fall morning, saying he'd be back in a while. Imagine that my mother hadn't asked, ''Where are you going?'' and he hadn't said, looking at his watch, as if time mattered, ''Nowhere special.''

Imagine, instead, that he opened the door and saw the bright fall trees, and said, ''Let's go for a ride with our baby.'' And that we drove down a country road, stopping to buy ice cream, and the two of them fed me bites from their cones and wiped the drool from my chin.

Imagine that we came home and ate. Imagine us all under a light, our faces shining. We are a family and will never be anything but a family, and Aunt Zis lives with us, and we are whole and perfect, the four of us.

I like the number four. It makes something solid and strong, like a table, a chair, a box. In a box there are four sides and four walls, and inside these four walls you can always feel safe.

''I'm having the worst trouble,'' Aunt Zis said suddenly. ''I can't remember what day it is.''

''Thursday,'' my mother said.

''Are you sure?'' Aunt Zis said.

''Uh-huh.''

''And what about Aaron?''

''What about him?'' I said.

Aaron is my mother's boyfriend. Big nose, pock-marked skin, and faded sweater vests covered with pipe ashes. Fifty-something. When I first met him I hated the way he mumbled around his pipe, and I kept wanting to shout at him, ''Straighten those shoulders!''

''What's Aaron's last name?'' Aunt Zis said. She sounded sort of tense.

11

"Kinnetz," I said. "Aaron Kinnetz."

"Jessie." My mother looked over her shoulder and let the car steer itself. A miracle we ever get anywhere safely. "I didn't realize Meadow's mother and I had so much in common," she said.

"You don't, Ma. What are you talking about?" Besides everything else, the Cowans skied in Switzerland and had a boat tied up at the marina.

"Kate Cowan's back in school," my mother said. "Working for a degree, too. We're a couple of middle-aged book crammers with kids. Of course, she's going for a master's and I'm still getting credits for freshman year. And she's got three little ones to care for, not counting Meadow. I only have you."

"*And* three jobs," I said. "Don't forget that little fact, Ma. Mrs. Cowan doesn't even have one job. She doesn't even clean her own house. You know what she does when they have a party—picks up the phone and hires people to do everything."

"Don't tell me any more!" my mother said. "Jessie, when you marry, marry a rich man."

"Maribeth!" Aunt Zis said. "I don't like to hear you talk like that."

"She can love a rich man as well as a poor man."

"She doesn't have to get married at all."

"Did I say that she did? All I said was . . ."

I leaned forward and put a hand on each of their shoulders—my aunt's light as a twig, my mother's thick with warm flesh—and sniffed the mingled familiar smells of them, tobacco, lemon shampoo, rose water cologne. Words floated into my mind. *Just this way . . . just this way* . . . Not four, I thought. Three. Not a square, a triangle. The three of us—joined, linked, solid. Three sides, not four.

✸

FOUR

Love-Hate Relationship

"I found a kitty on the way home yesterday," I said to Meadow. "Real little thing, all by itself in the weeds near an empty lot."

"Oh, poor thing!" Meadow said. "What'd you do?" We were in the back of her mother's van, on the way to the club the Cowans belonged to. We were going to meet Diane and play racquetball.

"I took him home, fed him. Egg and milk. Good, right? I wanted to keep him, I was already thinking about naming him. Oh, man, you should have seen my mother's face when she came home from work and heard that. I had to get on the phone and call the ASPCA right away to find out where to bring him."

"Why doesn't she like cats?" Meadow's eyebrows were two blond, outraged peaks. The Cowans had three longhair cats, uncountable numbers of gerbils and white mice, and two German shepherds. "I thought everyone loved cats."

"Well, that's a stupid thought."

"Jessie, I knew you were going to say that!"

"And I knew *you* were going to say *that*."

Meadow and I have been friends so long we're either

13

in perfect harmony or else we argue like a grouchy old married couple. Love-hate relationship. We know everything about each other—I could probably predict what brand of cereal she's going to eat tomorrow morning—and we talk about everything. Well, nearly everything.

I never talk about James Wells, not to anyone, not even Meadow. Years ago, I noticed how people's faces changed when they heard I didn't have a father, or, rather, that I did, but that I didn't know anything about him, not even where he was. Sometimes, the faces opened up like a bucket waiting for scraps to be thrown in. *A father who deserted his child* . . . And sometimes the faces seemed to slide away, almost melt, as if the eyes and ears didn't want to see and hear something so ugly.

"If we kept that kitten we would have had to take it to the vet," I said, defending my mother. "Which costs a lot of money, as you should know. But probably it doesn't matter to you." I unzipped Meadow's sports bag to check that she'd remembered to bring a racket for me. "Besides, Ma's in one of her poverty moods."

"What moods?"

"Poor. Poverty. Hello? She's feeling like we don't have any money to spare. Lots of bills and not enough bucks to go around."

I was momentarily furious, as if Meadow had forced the words out of me, as if it were a shameful thing not to have money or multiple cats, or all the things she had. Okay, include a father. I fingered the buckle in my jacket pocket, tracing out the pattern of initials, the long, loopy J, the rounded W. "Look what I have," I said suddenly, bringing it out.

Meadow examined it. "Cool. Your initials, too. Where'd you get it?"

"Oh, in the house," I said vaguely. I already regretted showing it to her. I took it back and zipped it into the pocket on my sleeve.

14

"Bus!" Meadow's little sister, Scout, suddenly yelled. She was up front in her car seat.

"Train! Plane!" Meadow's two little brothers yelled back. They had taken over the middle of the van.

"How many Cowans do you think are in the phone book?" I asked Meadow.

"How would I know?"

"I know how many Wellses are in the phone book. One hundred and sixty-three."

Meadow stared at me. "So what?"

"Nothing. It's an interesting fact. Don't you like interesting facts?"

"Not the way you do, Jessie. I don't read phone books."

It was true—sometimes at home I opened the phone book and flipped through it, looking at the rows of tiny names. Eventually I'd get to the back of the book, to the Ws, and then to the Wellses. The first time I'd seen our name there in bold letters, WELLS, at the top of the long column, I'd been about six years old. I'd shouted, "Ma, Ma, come quick! Here's our name in the phone book!"

I looked out the van window. It was snowing again, thick wet flakes that stuck to everything like heavenly glue. "It's not even good powder," Meadow complained.

We were going through a poor section of town, and I saw someone sleeping in a doorway, a lump under a raggedy blanket. I shouldn't have looked. My heart speeded up. What if my mother got sick, what if she couldn't work, what if we didn't have money, couldn't pay our bills, lost our house . . .

"Med, what would I do if something happened to my mother?"

"Like what?"

"What if she got sick? What if she had an accident? What if she died?"

15

"That's morbid. Why do you think about things like that?"

"My mother had melanoma, you know that. Cancer of the skin, when I was four years old. Besides, I can't help my thoughts."

"Yes, you can. You don't have to think about depressing things. Discipline your mind."

"Thank you, I'll whip it nightly and send it to bed without supper."

"Anyway, you can always come live with me."

"Really?" I didn't want her to say it just to be nice. "Do you mean it?"

"Yes!"

"What about your parents?"

"They wouldn't even notice another kid."

"I'd have to go skiing if I was part of your family."

"No problem. We'd teach you."

Meadow thinks if I only tried harder I could do all the things she does. When we met in kindergarten, she could already do the best cartwheels, somersaults, and leaps in the whole class. She also spoke the least of anyone and was the shyest person. Never, no matter how hard I tried, could I manage a cartwheel, but I always knew how to talk. My big talent. I became Meadow's voice. I was the one who carried her messages to the world. "Mrs. Lesesne, Meadow wants to be blackboard monitor. . . . No, Nicky! Meadow doesn't want to share her milk with you. . . . Mrs. Lesesne, Meadow needs a pencil. . . ."

"Is Diane going to be on time?" Meadow put her foot up on the seat and relaced her sneakers. Whenever she said Diane's name, there was a tiny edge to her voice.

Diane and I met last summer, at an acting class at the Y, downtown. When the teacher called for improv teams, we stood up at the same moment, as if we'd planned it. And we started talking and have never stopped.

"Didn't you say she was always late for things, Jessie? I don't like to waste court time. It really irritates me.''

I zipped and unzipped my sleeve pocket. Why did I keep trying to push Meadow and Diane together? I knew. It was that thing of wanting the friends you loved to love the friends you loved.

''There he is,'' Meadow said, ''the guy I told you about.'' We had just walked into the clubhouse, and she was looking at the blond kid with muscles behind the counter. He was wearing a tight white T-shirt with cut-off arms. ''Jack Kettle,'' she whispered.

''You want to talk to him?''

''No!'' She rushed me away, down the stairs, to the locker room. ''That was Jack Kettle,'' she said again.

''Who?'' Diane said. She was waiting for us, all ready to play in powder-blue sweats, her long black hair pulled up in a ponytail.

''Diane's on time!'' I said. ''How are you, baby doll?''

''On time and on a diet.'' She sucked in her cheeks.

''Dieting again. You *are* an idiot.'' I scrubbed her head.

''What's a Jack Kettle, Meadow?'' she asked.

''For most of us, Diane,'' I said, ''it's that blond bimbo guy with the overgrown muscles at the counter. But for Meadow—''

''Jessie,'' Meadow said warningly.

''—he's a big crush.''

''Is that like an Orange Crush?'' Diane said.

''Meadow has had some very cool crushes, Diane. Am I right, Med? But, this time, I don't think she's picked a winner.'' I hung my jacket in the locker. ''Jack Kettle hasn't got a single active brain cell to go with all those muscles. These guys who are obsessed with working out and going on the machines—''

''How do you know he's obsessed with working

17

out?'' Meadow said. "How do you know he goes on the machines? How do you know anything about him, Jessie? You never even saw him before today."

"Meadow, do I have to be dropped in the ocean to know it's wet? Do I have to burn my hand to know fire is hot?"

Shut up, I told myself, as I often did. And as I often did, I didn't. "Do I really have to see Jack Kettle in the flesh lifting weights to know where he got those puffy muscles?"

Meadow looked pained, or maybe just furious. She walked out of the locker room, slapping her racket against her leg.

"Well, let's get on the court, so Meadow can beat us up," I said. Now I felt guilty for going on about Jack Kettle just to amuse Diane.

"Is she a good player?" Diane said.

"You'll see."

We had the court for an hour and played three games of cutthroat. Meadow, playing against Diane and me, won the first game, 21–10. The second game, Diane made seven points. It was supposed to be her against me and Meadow, but Meadow might as well have been alone on the court. She went for every shot.

"That was certainly a relaxing game," I said, when we took a water break. "I should have brought my blankey and taken a nap. Did I make contact with even one ball?"

The last game, I played against Meadow and Diane. I started with confidence—after all, I wasn't a bad *bad* player, but Meadow killed my first shot against the front wall, and I didn't get the service back for twelve points. The final score was 21–3. Do I have to say who got three and who got twenty-one?

"I noticed your forehand is improving, Jessie," Meadow said, when we were in the showers. "Your big

18

weakness is your backhand. You should really practice your swing at home.''

Is there anything worse than being given advice you didn't ask for? Actually, yes. Being given advice you didn't ask for by the person who's just beaten you. Badly.

''You don't keep your eye on the ball,'' Meadow lectured. ''That's one of the most important things in any ball game.''

''Everlasting gratitude for the arcane information,'' I said, grabbing my towel.

''Oh, she's mad,'' Meadow said. ''She's mad about losing.''

''Hey, I am not. I love losing. It's so much fun.''

''Whenever Jessie's mad, Diane,'' Meadow said, ''she uses words no one understands. Arcane. Sounds dirty.''

I turned on the hair dryer. ''Relax, sweetie, it only means secret.''

''Oh, I know that,'' Meadow said.

''Sure you do.''

We were sneering at each other, but suddenly Meadow grabbed me and mashed our noses together so hard I grunted. ''Pig! Pig! Pig!'' she said.

Now I was supposed to say, ''Oink oink oink.'' In grade school this had been—don't ask me why—our make-up-the-fight routine.

''Pig pig pig,'' Meadow repeated.

''Oink oink oink,'' I said finally. I was mortified that Diane was watching this. But the truth was, as soon as I said it, I felt much better.

✿

FIVE

The D Zone

When I woke up, I saw my breath puffing into the air. I always sleep with the window open, so my bedroom is usually cool, but this morning it was freezing. I danced around on the cold floor, pulling on my jeans and a sweater. My fingers were actually stiff with cold. I ran down the hall; the whole house was like an ice cave. My mother's windows were silvered over with frost flowers. "Ma." I shook her through the tangle of blankets. "Get up."

She groaned. "Do I have to?"

"There's no heat in the house. It's dead cold. It's the North Pole. Did you hear me? Up, Maribeth."

My mother came out of bed like a bear and went charging down the stairs. "Are you crazy, Ma?" I said. "Put on socks!"

"My feet are always hot."

In the cellar, she thumped on pipes with a wrench and peered at gauges. "I don't know what the hell I'm doing," she said, and went back out to the kitchen.

Aunt Zis appeared. She was in her nightgown. "What's all the noise?" She sneezed four or five times.

"Zis, get back in bed," my mother said, picking up the phone to call the gas company.

"No heat, Aunt Zis." I got a blanket and wrapped it around her shoulders.

"We've got a child in this house!" my mother yelled into the phone. "And an elder citizen! What do you mean, shutting off our gas?" She listened. Then she said, "Okay, okay, okay."

"Okay what?" I asked when she hung up.

"Okay, nothing. This woman claims the bill hasn't been paid. She said they sent us a warning. Damn, I need some coffee."

But there was no gas to heat water. "What a way to start the day," my mother moaned. "All right, I want the numbers on the checks. Zis—"

Aunt Zis had already opened the drawer where we kept bills, receipts, and lottery tickets, all our financial stuff. She was the one who took care of the checkbook. She handed it to me. "You look, Jessie, my fingers are too stiff."

The last check to the gas company was over four months ago.

My mother picked out envelopes from the mess in the drawer. "The gas bills," she said.

"I don't understand," Aunt Zis said. "I pay the bills." Her hands were shaking.

"Oh, shoot, look at this," my mother said. She had a postcard. "It's the warning to pay. Didn't we have the money, Zis?"

My aunt held her hand to her mouth. "I think someone came . . . from the company. . . . He came to the door. I was going to tell you—"

"I better call and see what I have to do to get us some heat," my mother said.

I walked upstairs with my aunt. "I don't know how that happened. I never used to forget anything," she said. "I always had a wonderful memory."

"You still do. You have a great memory."

It wasn't true. For a while now, she'd been forgetting lots of little things, like what she went to the store to buy. And big things, like her doctor appointments. She never used to be like that. Maybe that was why we hadn't taken it too seriously.

She got back in bed and I covered her with an extra blanket. "Don't worry about that stupid bill." I stroked her head. "Who cares if we're cold for a few hours? It doesn't matter."

She clutched the covers to her chin, went deeper into the blankets, disappeared under them, until all I could see were her anguished eyes and a tiny bit of dry fluffy hair.

"Kids," Mr. Novak said, "this will be a joint social studies—language arts project for me and Mrs. Scher, connecting the events of the twentieth century with the lives of real people. The subject is family and history. *Your* family. Maybe you think your family doesn't have anything to do with history, but we don't agree."

He stroked his soft blond beard. "Most of the history you learn in school is the history of great leaders and great events—wars, disasters, discoveries. But there's something else—there're the people who live through these events. Dig into your family history, their memories and stories."

The wind was blowing hard outside, rattling the windows. Cold air crept around my legs. I was having trouble concentrating. I wished I'd stayed home with Aunt Zis.

"It's up to you how you do this project," Mr. Novak said. "It could be a linear history of your family. It could be the story of how your family got to this country. Maybe you'll focus on a particular person in your family, such as someone who went through the Depression or the Korean War."

"Huh?" Bob Doolan said from across the room.

"You're going to find out stuff you never knew when you start asking questions and looking into things. This should be a lot of fun for you people."

Someone whispered, someone else yawned, someone's knees whammed into a desk. The usual sounds.

"Mrs. Scher and I want something unique from each of you. No going to the dictionary and copying out a definition of family. That's going to get you nowhere fast."

Bob Doolan raised his hand. "What's unique?"

"It's singular, it's distinctive. You're not looking too happy with that, Mr. Doolan. Think of it this way, what's unique is yours, it can't be anybody else's, like your famous *Huh?*"

That was a signal for everybody to laugh and move around, yawn some more.

"Okay, calm down," Mr. Novak said. "Let's get back to this now, it's important. Your half-term mark is going to be based on this report. You have six weeks, plenty of time, so no excuses about the canary ate your computer. Remember, every family has a story and every story is different."

He was giving me the eye, as if he knew my family story. Fleeing father. Abandoned child. Heartbroken mother. Dramatic stuff. The Oprah show. Geraldo. *Sorry to disappoint you, Mr. Novak, but I'm not writing about that stuff. Especially not about the human being who is or was my father. How much can you say about an absence, an emptiness, a vacant space?*

"Each family has a different makeup," Mr. Novak was saying, "a different history. Remember that word *unique*?"

I was fading out again. Wasn't every moment in life unique? How did you know which unique moments made a unique family history? Suppose sitting here in this classroom was unique. Suppose seeing Aunt Zis depressed this morning was unique. Suppose James Wells's deserting us was unique. Were they all equally unique?

"Did you say something, Miss Wells?" Mr. Novak asked.

I shook my head. I hoped he wouldn't ask me to repeat the last thing he'd said. Something about how the report could be written, verbal, visual . . . or whatever.

I stuck my legs out into the aisle and wrote my mother's name, mine, and my aunt's in my notebook. Maribeth, Jessie, Elizabeth. Could I tell the unique story of how "Elizabeth" got to be "Aunt Zis"? How my baby brain figured out that she had appeared as a replacement for my father, and when my mother reminded me that she was my aunt, I said stubbornly, "No, Ma, sister," only I pronounced it *zister*. I insisted on zister, my mother insisted on aunt. At some point, I said "Aunt Zister," and my mother gave in. It was one of our favorite family stories.

Great, but what did that have to do with history? *Not much, dummy.* Another D word.

I'd been collecting them. D words were dominant in doom and gloom. Dismal, dreary, disappointing, discouraging, disheartening, dispiriting, depressing. Had enough? Discard, disappear, destroy, destruction, dead, death, disease, decay . . . Welcome to the D zone.

I was still thinking about the assignment when I was setting the table that night. Aaron was coming to dinner and I was using my favorite dishes, which were cream colored, with a design of tiny blue flowers. What I especially liked was how they were crisscrossed with spidery lines of age, as if they had been with us forever. Faithful dishes. I could write about them. *My great-great-great-grandmother was given these dishes on her wedding day in faraway Hungary. She was seventeen years old. When her seventeen-year-old daughter married, my great-great-great-grandmother passed them on to her. And when her daughter married, after World War I, she brought them with her to this country.*

It sounded like a unique concept to me—history through plates and cups. There was just one problem— my mother and I had bought the dishes at a garage sale. I went into the kitchen for napkins. The front door slammed. "I'm home," my mother yelled. She came in and dropped her packages on the counter. "Hi, sweetie. What's up? Where's Zis?"

"She's still in bed. Ma, she's so upset about that gas bill—"

"I know." My mother sat down. "I wish I'd caught it before it was shoved in her face." She rubbed her calves. "My legs are like spaghetti. Brenda had me chasing up and down to the attic all afternoon with boxes of files."

"She should pay you more. You work so hard for her."

"One of these days." She put an unlit cigarette in her mouth. She had that sunken look around her eyes that meant, *Help, I need my nicotine fix.*

"Don't smoke in the house," I said.

"I never smoke in the house."

"You do too."

"Only in my room, with the windows open."

"When are you going to quit?"

"Not today! I have enough stress. Look, my pockets are empty! I cleaned us out paying the gas bill." She pulled out the pockets of her jeans, in one of her dramatic gestures, and paper clips and coins rained over the floor.

"I thought you got paid from the stable the other day."

"It all went on the car," she said. "It's disgusting."

"Well, did Brenda pay you?"

"She will, she's having some problems of her own right now. Her son—"

"Ma! You're not a charity bureau. Does she owe you a lot? I'm going to call her and tell her to pay you."

"Jessie, don't you do that."

"I'll ask Aaron for money when he comes."

"Don't you dare." She started putting food away. "Find out if Aunt Zis is coming down for dinner. And call Aaron, see if he's on his way."

"How did you decide on your life work, Aaron?" I said later, at dinner. He's a real estate broker and works for himself in a little office that looks like a dustbin.

He tapped his breast pocket, where he kept his pipe. "My life work?"

Hearing the pompous little phrase repeated, I winced. "I meant, how did you get going in real estate?" I'm always fascinated by how people decide to do whatever it is they do. Why do they make this choice and not that? How do they know if it's right or wrong? Did my father think about it before he walked out that morning, or did he just go?

". . . wasn't something I actually chose," Aaron mumbled.

When Aaron speaks, he hardly moves his lips. It's kind of distracting. At least I'm not distracted by his appearance anymore. Now I think he just looks sort of comfortable, like a big easy chair.

". . . dreams of being an architect," he was saying. "I wanted to design buildings and—God bless," he interrupted himself to say to Aunt Zis, who'd just sneezed. Then he mumbled something else that sounded like "wanted to leave my park on the furled."

"Mark on the world," my mother translated.

"What Aaron really means—," Aunt Zis said, and we all turned to look at her. She hadn't said a word all

26

through the meal. "—is that when he dies, he wants a *big, fat* obituary in the newspaper."

My mother and I looked at each other and laughed. Aunt Zis sounded like herself again.

I sat on the window seat with the phone book in my lap, opened to the Ws, actually to the Wellses. It was snowing again. Outside, it was dark and light: dark night, dark houses, white snow, light-filled windows. I started counting the J Wellses.

J. Wells, Jacob Wells, three Jameses, Jayne, one Joby, one Jody, a bunch of Johns, and one Jules. Thirteen people with the initials JW. What if one of them was related to James Wells? But why stop there? There were another hundred and fifty Wellses. Maybe one of *them* was related to James Wells and even knew something about him. Such as, where he was. Which meant I could know, too.

In the dark window my reflection seemed to float in the falling snow. *I could know, too.* I was stunned by this idea, and even more stunned that I'd never thought of it before.

❀

SIX

My Little Secret

I like to memorize things. I like studying maps. Things like that don't make a difference in your life that you can feel or eat or see, but I think it helps you have an idea about the world. Helps me, anyway. I like knowing England is an island and Italy is shaped like a boot. It's knowledge, something else that's your own, even if it doesn't have a practical use. That weekend, I memorized the phone numbers of all the J. Wellses. That wasn't practical, either.

I wasn't planning on doing anything with the phone numbers, but Monday after I came home from school, I sat down on the window seat in the hall and dialed the first number on the list. Our house was quiet. Aunt Zis was out for a walk, and Ma wouldn't be home from work at the diner until late.

J. Wells's phone rang ten times, and then I hung up. Jacob Wells was next, but as I was starting to dial, I thought, *Why don't I just begin at the beginning*?

A. R. Wells didn't answer, either. Nor did A. W. Wells. I wrote DA in tiny letters next to their names and dialed Andrew Wells. The phone was picked up right away. "Byrnes Vacuum Service. What can I do for ya?"

"Is Andrew Wells there?"

"This is Byrnes Vacuum Service."

"Is this 555-3421?"

"Yes. What can I do for ya?"

"Is Andrew Wells there?"

"Hey, what is this, a prank call?" *Bang.* I was cut off.

After that, it was Mrs. Burl Wells, who answered on the second ring with a cheerful "Hel-lo!"

"Mrs. Wells, my name is Jessie Wells." My knee began aching. "You don't know me, but I wanted to ask—that is, I was hoping you could help me. That is, either you or Mr. Wells. That is—," I heard myself saying for the third time, and I stopped and took a breath. "Mrs. Wells, I'm trying to find out if Mr. Wells could be related to my, um, to James Wells."

"Oh, no, I'm sure he's not, and I'll tell you why. There is no Mr. Wells."

"He's gone?" I blurted.

"There is no *he* to be gone."

"Excuse me?"

"It's my little secret, but I'll share it. I am Mr. Burl Wells *and* Mrs. Burl Wells. I think a lady living alone is safer if people believe she's not living alone. You understand? My name is Beryl, so Burl is very close, you see."

"Do you think James Wells is related to you?"

"Oh, no, Wells isn't my given name. That was so hard to pronounce, I shortened it years ago. I can hardly even remember it myself anymore," she said happily.

Next I got C. J. Wells's son, who said he knew for a fact they had no relatives named James. Casper Wells was an old man with a hearing problem. When he finally understood what I wanted, he said, "Barking up the wrong tree," and hung up. Corrine Wells answered on the second ring. "What?" she kept saying in a soft Southern accent. "Is this a joke, honey? Is this a new

29

way to raise money? You just tell me if it is."

"No, really, I'm trying to find out about my father."

"Well, I'll trust you, honey, but I'm afraid I have to disappoint you. My husband's a colonel in the army, and we just got posted up here. We're both from North Carolina, that's where all his Wells relatives live, honey."

Crane Wells's number rang twice, then a mechanical voice informed me that the number had been disconnected and the listing removed from the directory. I couldn't speak to Dr. Curlene Wells, but her nurse promised to put my question to her. "I doubt it, though," she said. "Dr. Wells just moved here two years ago from Chicago, where I understand her family has always lived."

I'd hardly made a dent in the list, and I was getting bored or tired. Something. Maybe just another D word— discouraged. One more, I told myself. I drummed my fingers on the windowsill. Three rings. Four. Five. Here we go. "Hello, you don't know me, my name is Jessie Wells, and I was wondering . . ."

SEVEN

Unmentionable Acts

Meadow wanted to call Jack Kettle. That is, she wanted me to call, but not say who I was or who I was calling for. "I'm past the stage of making anonymous calls to boys, Med, and you should be, too."

"Jessie!" Her pale face flamed. "You know how I am."

"Shy." I sighed.

"Massively shy." She opened my closet and took out a pink shirt. "Did I give this to you?"

"A million years ago. It's too small for me now. You want it back?"

"No. Throw it away."

"Nothing doing. I'll save it for my daughter."

"You probably will, too."

"Listen, Med, if you go on the Save-the-County Walk with me next month, I'll call Jack Kettle for you today."

"Nothing doing. I'm not walking twenty miles, or whatever it is, for one measly phone call."

"Okay, call Jack Kettle yourself. You just think you can't do it, but you can. It's all in your mind. You're the one who's so big on disciplining your mind."

"This is different, Jessie!"

"You could talk to him at the clubhouse, you know."

"Do *what*?" She sounded as if I had recommended she commit an unmentionable act.

"How about I call, but you talk to him?"

"Jessie, I can't."

"Right. The dread three-letter word. S. H. Y."

"It's not a joke. It's the worst thing in the world."

"The worst thing in the world? How about being hungry? How about not having a home?"

"Are you going to make the call or not?"

"How about I break the ice, then—"

"No."

"How about you just say hello?"

"No."

"How about you grow up?"

"That's not funny. You don't get it, because you're not shy."

"I *do* get it." I did, I was sure I did. Still, after all these years, how come she hadn't figured out how easy it was to talk to people? Talk, and they talked to you. All you had to do was say what you wanted to say and do what you wanted to do. *Like James Wells did? Wanted to walk out, so he walked out. Wanted to leave, so he left. Didn't want to know you, so he didn't.*

Heat ran up in my face. "Okay, let's go call Jack Kettle," I said. We went out to the hall for the phone. "He's not going to be home," I warned Meadow. "Not this time on a Saturday." I'm so smart. One ring, and I heard a male voice saying, "Kettle house. Jack speaking."

Meadow made a victory sign and moved closer so she could hear everything.

"How fortunate I found you in, Jack." I dropped my voice to make it more interesting. "I have a message for you. Someone thinks you are *trés* interesting."

"You mean you?"

"If I meant myself, I would say so."

"Who's this someone?"

"I can't tell you that, Jack. I will tell you that you've seen her where you work." Meadow drove her sharp little chin warningly into my shoulder. "You've seen her here, you've seen her there," I added.

"You sound cute."

I glanced at Meadow. "Jack, I'm not your type."

"I like your voice."

"Why?"

"It's a good voice."

"What is a bad voice? Is this a voice we punish?"

He laughed. "This other girl, what does she look like? Is she pretty?"

"Is that all that matters to you, Jack? Don't you have anything else on your mind? However, if you must know, yes, she's pretty. Blond, big brown eyes, plus she's smart and athletic."

"She's blond? Why doesn't she talk to me herself?"

"What difference does her hair color make? Anyway, she's not ready to talk to you yet."

"What's her name?"

"Now, now, Jack. You know that's a secret. I'll give you her first initial. M."

"Meagan Farber?"

"Don't you wish." Meagan was a senior who'd been prom queen last year and who, everyone said, was a shoo-in for valedictorian this year.

"Mary Mercer? Misty Alzicia? Mavis—"

"Three guesses and you're out."

"—Kaplin?"

"Bye-bye, Jack." I put the phone down.

"You shouldn't have said that about the clubhouse," Meadow said. "You gave him a big clue."

"You're griping! That's the thanks I get for doing your dog work?"

"What do you want me to do?"

"Grovel at my feet. Say I'm a wonderful friend."

33

"You're a wonderful friend."

I smiled modestly. "I know."

Later that day, I went over to Diane's. She was tired. "I couldn't sleep last night," she said. "I kept waking up and thinking and feeling awful—"

"What was so awful?" She did look sort of dragged out.

"I don't want to talk about it. I feel weak, and I'm eating too much. I ate three bananas and a quart of ice cream, and I'm still famished. I want to eat the kitchen!"

We got food to take to her room, and on the way up, I checked out The Stuff, which is what I call all the little interesting things that are everywhere in the McArdle house. Bowls and vases, and hand-carved boxes and strings of beads made from shells and stones. The Stuff. All the things Diane's parents collected during the years they taught overseas. The first time Diane mentioned the places she'd been with her family—Morocco, Kenya, Indonesia—my arms broke out in welts from excitement.

In her room, Diane collapsed on her bed. "My body is mad at me." She dug into the bag of chips. "I have to eat to keep up my strength."

"Do you sleep with the window open?" I asked.

Diane shuddered. "In this weather? I know, I know. You do. Not me! I'd never get any sleep that way."

Her brother, Charlie, poked his head in the door. "What are you guys doing?" he asked.

"We *guys* are talking," I said.

"Girl talk?" Charlie smiled. Even though he was a year older, I always thought of him as younger. He had a sort of big-eared, little-boy look. Quite adorable.

"Girl talk, right," Diane said. "Get out." She threw a pillow at the door.

I examined the pictures on her bureau—snaps of her parents, her brother, bunches of relatives, and Kevin, her boyfriend. "Kevin's cute, Diane, I love his big glasses."

"Me too." She yawned.

"Diane, what's your theory on why I've never been kissed?"

"Youth and immaturity, my child."

"Thanks, Mom. How many times have you been kissed?"

"So many I've lost track."

She was yawning again. To wake her up, I told her about the call to Jack Kettle, and I complained about Meadow, which I shouldn't have done, but I did. "I wish she'd get a crush on someone more worthwhile."

Diane held a pillow against her chest. "Come on, Jessie, give her a break. You're so hard on her."

"What?" My eye twitched nervously and I got that flash of heat in my cheeks. Was that true? *Sure is*, a voice said in my ear ... my head ... my mind. ... A man's voice. *His* voice. *Scratched the belt buckle ... not exactly a light touch ... pretty damn hard on everything.* ... I shook my head, like clearing it of water.

Diane was saying something about the orchestra. "I was so nervous. My first trumpet solo."

"You and Meadow are talented. I'm a musical idiot."

"My father says everyone has talent. He says when he went to school, all the kids got music lessons free. That was in a little town near the Vermont border."

"I thought he grew up in South Carolina."

"That's my mother. My grandfather was an artist, and he wanted to live in the country. They were the only black family in town. My father says they were such a big tribe, they never got lonely. There were seven kids. He says it was great growing up there."

I sat down next to her on the bed and started braiding her hair. "I'm jealous of you. Your family is so big—"

"Well, I'm jealous of you, so we're even."

"You're not jealous of me. I don't believe that." I pulled the braid apart and brushed her hair smooth with my fingers. "What could you possibly be jealous of?"

"Your spontaneous self. I worry too much about my dignity. I guard myself. I know I do. I should be more relaxed and open."

"Diane, you're nuts. You're perfect the way you are."

Sasha, her golden retriever, who was lying at the foot of the bed, whined up and down the scale. "See, Diane, Sasha agrees with me. You're perfect."

"Oh, yes, perfect Diane McArdle. Straight A's, cheerleader, wears up-to-the-minute clothes, and practices her music at least an hour a day."

I held out the hairbrush like a microphone. "Tell our audience, Ms. McArdle, how it feels to be a perfect person."

"It makes you feel sick."

"Perfectly sick, I presume?"

"Your stomach is in knots, you want to throw up. You're always afraid *what if you can't do it*. And even when things happen in your own family and you feel bad, you can't cry or you'll upset them. They want you to understand and be perfect and upbeat and cheerful all the time, and sometimes *I can't stand it*." She was breathing hard. She wiped her eyes with her hand and turned her face away.

"Diane?" I said uncertainly. I felt like someone who'd walked into a room expecting a party and found a hospital ward. I didn't understand what had just happened. Was someone in her family sick? Had something happened, something unmentionable? "Diane?" I said again.

She sat up and took a sandwich and started tearing the crusts off. "I hate crusts," she said. "Don't you?" Her voice was vehement, but her face was shut down tight as a closed door.

✳

EIGHT

Jealous Eyes

"Brush harder, sweetie," my mother said, slapping Domino on the rump. "Don't be afraid, this little baby is not going to mind. She likes it."

"I'm not afraid of her," I lied. Domino was a spotted gray mare. I brushed harder. I liked her smell, and I liked the smell of the stables, but I wasn't at ease around horses.

"I wonder if Alicia is around today," my mother said. "I bet she'd let you ride."

My mother was always excited when her boss said I could take one of the horses, but for me, riding was a grit-your-teeth act of courage.

She picked up the wall phone to call up to the main house. "I think I'll ask her if you—"

"Ma!" I held her arm. "I have something I want to tell you. I'm calling the Wellses." I hadn't planned to say it.

"You're doing what?"

"Calling all the Wellses. Everyone in the phone book with the same last name as us."

"Why?" She put the phone back on the hook.

"Maybe one of them is related to James Wells."

"I'll tell you right now. No."

"How do you know that? Are you sure?"

"I don't want you to do this, Jessie." She slapped her pockets, looking for a cigarette, even though she couldn't smoke in the barn. "Hey, if you're going to do that, why stop with our phone book? This could be a lifetime project, you could call the Wellses in Minneapolis, Los Angeles, Dallas. Every city in the country."

"Okay, maybe it's stupid," I said. "Is that what you're telling me? It's stupid? Just say it. It's stupid, Jessie!"

"I didn't say that. Just"—she pushed her hands through the air—"useless. You're wasting your time."

I brushed Domino, long hard strokes, pushing my forehead against her flank. "What if one of those people knows where James Wells is?"

"Jess, don't do it." My mother forked straw and manure into the wheelbarrow. "Nothing will come of it but grief."

"How do you know that? Why? I don't understand what you're saying."

"There're a lot of things you don't know."

"What does that mean? What don't I know?"

"Could you just take my word and not do it?" She put her hands around my face and looked at me steadily. "I love you, sweetie. You're the most important thing in the world to me."

"I love you, too, Mom," I mumbled.

She pushed the wheelbarrow to the next stall. Now she was saying something about Aaron and dinner at his house next week. Her voice was muffled by the wall between us. I heard the steady scrape of the shovel against the cement floor.

I started working on Domino again. I tried to push the conversation with my mother out of my mind. I thought about horses instead. I thought about how sweetly Domino stood there and let me brush her and bump into her, and then I thought about wild horses, herds of them racing in freedom, manes flying, raising dust, splashing through water. The wild ponies of Chincoteague. I'd always wanted to go there and see them. Even if I was uneasy around horses, I still loved them for their beauty, their independence, their big, intelligent faces.

Nobody tells them what to do. But that wasn't true. Maybe my mother was right. Calling one hundred and sixty-three Wellses was ridiculous. Like looking for a needle in a haystack. *My husband's folks are all from the South . . . barking up the wrong tree . . . that's not even my name, dear. . . .*

Even if I did find someone related to James Wells, what difference would it make? I'd still be in the same place I'd always been. The place of no father, the place of know nothing, the place of *who cared, anyway*.

My hands felt swollen and stiff, and the brush lagged down Domino's flank. She stamped her feet suddenly, as if she knew how I felt and she didn't like it. I stepped back until she got calm. Then I started brushing her again, thinking how strange it was that you could know everything about an animal's parents, but nothing about your own.

"Have you done anything on that family history assignment for Mr. Novak?" Meadow asked as we got on the bus.

"No." I didn't want to talk about it. Nothing I'd thought of seemed good enough. We walked to the back and took a seat.

We were on our way to the mall to meet Diane and watch Aunt Zis and her tap group dance. They were raising money for flood victims.

"Want one of my ideas?" Meadow asked.

"Our families are nothing alike."

"Well, you have to do something," she said. "You

39

don't have that much time left. I'm interviewing my father about his uncle—"

"I don't have a father. End of subject." I looked out the window. Heaps of dirty snow everywhere. "Don't talk to me, I feel really irritable," I said, and a moment later we exploded into a fight.

Meadow was acting thrilled, because she'd read that a movie star was coming here. "We might get to see him," she said. "Oh my god."

"Your tongue is hanging out," I said.

"Excuse me, Jessie? I was just expressing enthusiasm."

"You're always getting heated up over guys. Jack Kettle. This what's-his-face. If it's male, you think it's wonderful."

"Shut up, Jessie! What are you smiling about? You look like a Halloween pumpkin. What am I doing on this bus with you, anyway?"

"Going to give Aunt Zis moral support," I said sweetly.

"Aunt Zis," she spit out, "is an old fart."

My heart started beating really hard. "Meadow, take that back, or you just shot yourself down."

"I'm so scared." She flipped her long hair behind her ears. The bus ground to a stop, and she rushed off ahead of me.

"Don't think I'm forgetting that, Meadow," I said to her back. "What a rotten thing to say." My voice cracked. "And you know how much Aunt Zis likes you, too."

"Don't be so sensitive," she said. "Can't you take a joke? I didn't mean anything by it."

"Like hell you didn't. You showed your true colors. Rat colors."

She turned and bared her little teeth in my face. "Sometimes I hate your guts, Jessie."

We crossed the bridge to the mall. Diane was waiting

for us by the south entrance. "Hi, you two!"

"Hiii!" Meadow gave her an excessive hug. I walked ahead and found my aunt and the dance group near the fountain, where a "stage" had been marked off with yellow tape. A crowd had gathered. Aunt Zis noticed me and wagged a finger.

"Hi, sweetie," I said. A tall old man was soloing, skinny legs cutting the air like scissors.

"This is fun," Diane said, hugging my arm.

"I know," I agreed, but everything seemed wrong to me, fake and false. That Meadow and I weren't talking, that we were both covering up in front of Diane, that Diane had been *so* unhappy the other day and was *so* cheerful today. There was even something wrong about Aunt Zis, the way her legs were going, her feet tapping the floor. Was this the same Aunt Zis who'd crept up the stairs the morning the gas had been cut off?

"What's that music they're dancing to?" Diane said. "I should know it."

" 'Good Ship Lollipop,' " a woman standing next to us said. "Shirley Temple danced to it. She sang it, too." She eyed the three of us. I felt Meadow sort of slide behind me, out of range. "Shirley Temple was the most famous child in the world," the woman said. "She sang and danced like an angel. She was a talented actress. There was nothing that golden-haired child couldn't do. Talent, talent, talent, loaded with talent, persistence, and perseverance."

The woman stared at me, as if she knew all about me, knew I didn't have even a sprinkle of talent, not to mention my total lack of persistence. I'd given up so easily on calling the Wellses. I thought I had so much spirit, so much grit and independence. It was all a false front. One word from my mother and I'd let it drop.

"My first tap dance teacher was Helene Audrey Van Sternberg," Aunt Zis said. We'd taken a table in the food court. "She lived across the hall from us. She was eleven years old and gave lessons in the kitchen."

"Why the kitchen, Aunt Zis?" Meadow asked.

I took a bite from my raspberry ice-cream cone. Now she was being sweet? Another phony thing.

"Where else would she give lessons?" Aunt Zis said. "There was no such thing as a living room, not with nine people in three rooms. The kitchen was where everything happened. The children did their homework there, everyone ate there, and they had their fights there, and the bathtub was in there, too."

"The bathtub?" Diane said. "In the kitchen?"

"Cast-iron with a wooden board over it. Two of the little Van Sternbergs slept on that."

Diane collapsed against me. "Did you hear that, Jessie?"

Meadow was watching us, biting on a strand of hair. She had miserable, jealous eyes. Was she jealous enough to do something bad, like end our friendship? Like disappear out of my life? My stomach lurched. I took a long drink of my soda and made my mind pull away. I know how to do that—it's something I found out a long time ago. It's like stepping out of a room, then turning around and watching what's going on inside. I thought about Meadow and me as if I were thinking about two other people. *That's the way it is . . . people disappear . . . it happens all the time . . . and if it does, well . . . then it does.*

NINE

Buckets of Sound, Lakes and Oceans

"I'm glad you could join us, Jessie," Mrs. McArdle said, looking at me in the rearview mirror. She was driving.

"Thank you for asking me." First my mother, then Aunt Zis, had made me promise I'd say that. I would have anyway. I pulled my hair back behind my ears and sat up straighter, wishing I'd worn something better. All the McArdles were dressed up. Mr. McArdle was wearing a black bow tie with his suit. Both Diane and her mother were wearing long skirts and silk blouses, and Diane's hair was twisted up into a thick knot. Compared to her, I looked like I was going to a grade-school dance.

We were on the way to the Civic Center to see an opera called *The Magic Flute*. I had Charlie's ticket. I'd never been to an opera before, and I didn't know what to expect. "Why didn't your brother want to go?" I asked.

"He says he doesn't like opera," Diane said.

"Charlie's the independent type," Mr. McArdle said, from the front seat.

"He's also mad at my parents," Diane whispered.

"How come?"

"Oh, he's got his reasons. Dad." Diane leaned forward. "Do you know this is Jessie's first opera?"

Mr. McArdle turned to smile at me. He had a shining bald head with a thick fringe of black hair. "I wish I was going to my first opera. I was fifteen, and my grandfather took me. He didn't take my sisters, and to this day they have no interest in opera. My grandfather had a magnificent voice, almost another Paul Robeson. Do you know who he was, Jessie?"

I shook my head.

"A great singer," Diane said.

"And actor," her father said. "And athlete. And scholar. A fabulous human being. A black prince. One of those men God endows with brains, strength, beauty, and talent."

"Wow," I said, because I didn't know what else to say.

"Tonight you're going to hear the music of another prince. Wolfgang Amadeus Mozart. Maybe this will be the beginning of a love of opera for you, too, Jessie. I hope so. When we leave, you tell me what you think, okay?"

He gave me another smile, and I made up my mind that even if I was bored to tears, I'd tell him I loved it.

In the auditorium, Diane and I sat together, between her parents. Every seat was taken. The orchestra was tuning up, and a deep buzz of voices filled the hall. There was a kind of excitement in the air that I could almost reach out and touch. It was totally different from going to the movies, or even from plays and musicals I'd seen in school. But when the curtain went up, I was disappointed to see an almost bare stage with just a few pieces of fake-looking scenery.

"Here comes Tamino, the prince," Mr. McArdle whispered to me.

Some prince! Not like the one Mr. McArdle described in the car. This was a chubby guy in green tights and a green tunic, who was trying to avoid a monster who wouldn't have scared a two-year-old. After a while, three women warriors holding spears came onstage, and they were chubby, too. Everyone was singing and speaking in German, so I couldn't understand a word. Diane and her parents didn't seem to care. They all looked rapt, and when the women warriors finished off the monster and Tamino fainted, they and the whole audience roared with laughter. Okay, it was cute, but not *that* funny.

The warrior women were singing, having an argument, I thought, about who would get their mitts on Prince Tamino, when suddenly the stage darkened. Drums rumbled, the music soared, and in a flash of white light, a woman appeared in a glittering black gown.

"That's the Queen of the Night, Jessie," Mr. McArdle whispered.

She opened her mouth and sang, and if I hadn't had chills already, I would have got them then. From that moment, I was caught. I forgot the bare stage and the silly plot. All I knew was the way I felt listening to those voices, pouring out sound. Buckets of sound, lakes and oceans. Music, so much music, as if the world had been turned into music.

When we were leaving, Mr. McArdle said, "So, Jessie, what did you think?"

"I liked it," I said. "I loved it."

He looked happy, and in the car, we were all happy together, like one family. Diane put her arms around her parents. "I'm out with both my parents!" She kissed one, then the other. "I love you guys."

"I love you, too, sweetheart," her father said. "You are so precious to me."

It was like hearing the music again. It was like a song to Diane. *I love you, sweetheart . . . you are precious to me. . . .* Had James Wells ever said anything like that to me? Probably not. Or definitely not. Because if he had, he would never have walked out on me, would he?

TEN

Take Two Aspirin and Cheer Up

The brakes squealed as Maribeth slowed for a stop sign. Something always squealed, squeaked, or rattled on our car. "Let me out," I said. "I want to go home."

"What's the matter?"

"Nothing." My eyes hurt, my throat ached. A virus, PMS, or the fight with Meadow? We still weren't talking. All I wanted to do was curl up and feel sorry for myself.

"What movie did you say we were going to?" Aunt Zis said.

My stomach clenched. "We're not going to the movies, Aunt Zis. We're going to Aaron's for dinner."

There was a tiny moment of silence. "I thought he might be showing a home movie," she said.

Fast thinking. If I hadn't been feeling so crummy, I would have patted her on the back. Or laughed. Or cried. Diane said that for two days before her period, she cried at the drop of a hat. Meadow wouldn't even mention her period; she thought it was gross to talk about things like that.

I sneezed. "Getting a cold?" my mother said. "Take—"

47

"I know, take two aspirin and cheer up." My mother hardly ever got sick, and when she did, she didn't get in bed like a normal person. She soldiered on, and she expected everyone else to do the same. Maybe I had pneumonia. Take two aspirin and cheer up. Maybe it was already too late, and I was going to die. Take two aspirin and cheer up.

"I don't want to eat at Aaron's house," I said. "I didn't accept his invitation. You did."

"Why is she acting like this?" my mother said to Aunt Zis. "I thought she'd be glad to be invited."

Why was my mother talking about me as if I weren't there?

Because you're not. Because you don't exist. Because the person sitting in the backseat is a clone from another universe. The Universe of Bad Moods.

We drove through dark streets. Aaron's apartment was on the edge of downtown, and everything was dark and shuttered. Not a soul in sight. I slumped lower in the seat and half-closed my eyes. The wheels hummed monotonously over the pavement.

And then a strange thing occurred.

Something—someone—seemed to settle in next to me. I felt the seat give a little, a kind of stiff bounce, as if someone were making himself comfortable, and I heard a sound, almost a growl, in my ear . . . my head . . . my mind. . . . *Think you're the only one who has problems . . . the only one who's got it tough . . .*

I leaned into the corner. "You don't know me," I whispered fiercely. I waited for an answer. I heard the wind slide by the window, heard the murmur of my mother's and Aunt Zis's voices. Nothing else.

✦

ELEVEN

Say It with Conviction

"How long are we going to do this?" I said, falling into step with Meadow.

"Do what?"

"Be mad at each other. I bet you don't even know anymore why you're mad at me."

"I do too!" Her guitar case banged against her leg.

"I'm over being mad. Why aren't you? Are you jealous of Diane? Now don't get mad. I'm just asking an honest question."

She shrugged. "Maybe I am, and maybe I should be How come you and Diane never fight? How come you're always so happy with each other?"

"That's not true, Meadow. Anyway, Diane and I don't see each other much, so it's a honeymoon when we do."

"You make me so mad sometimes, Jessie! Honeymoon? What are you, lovers?"

"You make me mad, too, with stupid remarks like that. But so what, I always love you."

"Me too," she snapped.

We stared tensely at each other. "Are we making up or not?" I demanded. "Yes or no? Say what you mean and say it with conviction."

49

"Yes! I'm saying it with conviction. Will you shut up now?"

"Never. Just one thing, you have to take back what you said about Aunt Zis."

"You know I do. I took it back the minute I said it."

"Okay, then, we're made up. Anyway, you can't get rid of me, we've been friends too long."

"Creep." Meadow slapped me rapidly several times on the arms. "Who said I wanted to get rid of you? Let's go call Jack Kettle. That's the way you can really make up with me."

We crossed the street to a phone booth. "I saw him the other night when Mom and Dad played in the tennis tournament," she said. She dialed and quickly handed me the phone.

"Heeey. It's the girl with the voice," Jack Kettle said.

"Heeey, it's the boy with the laugh."

He laughed.

"So, do you want to talk about pollution and over-population, Jack? You want to talk about serious things?"

He laughed again.

"Did you ever think, Jack, that our planet is like a huge sprawling house, and we humans are like the family that moved in and forgot to pay the rent?"

"Heeey."

"When we moved in, we had more rooms than we knew what to do with. More rooms than we'd ever need, *so we thought*. Which is why we didn't bother cleaning up our messes. If a room got too grotty, well, hey, we just trekked on to a nice fresh room. We had so many rooms we'd never even seen them all."

"What are you doing?" Meadow hissed.

I held up my hand. "A long time passed, Jack, and the family was having some problems. The plumbing wasn't the greatest anymore, the roof was leaking, and people were starting to notice that just about every room in the house was in use, including some of the old dirty rooms.''

I paused to give him a chance to say something. He was silent. ''What do you think about all this, Jack?''

''He doesn't think anything,'' Meadow said. ''He's gone.'' She had her finger pressed down on the switch. ''You were boring him, Jessie. I know, because you were boring me.'' She picked up her guitar case and walked away.

I went after her. ''Meadow, are you mad again?''

''There wasn't anything about me in that conversation.''

''You don't want me to mention your name, you don't want me to say how you look, you don't want me to say that you know him from the clubhouse. What am I supposed to say?''

''I don't know,'' Meadow said. She looked forlorn. I threw my arms around her. ''Jessie,'' she said. ''I missed you all week.''

I hugged her. ''I missed you, too.''

We walked over to Allen Avenue, where her guitar teacher lived, and we talked about everything that had happened to us that week. I told her about the opera and PMS, but I didn't say that in the car that night, I thought I heard James Wells speak to me. I couldn't say it. Even if I had been in the habit of talking about him, I wouldn't have said it. Who would ever believe it, except me—or God?

TWELVE

✱

Somebody Good Like Me

Just as I got home from school on Tuesday, the phone rang and a raspy voice said, "I have your aunt. Is this Jessie? This is Victor Perl. I'm a total stranger, but don't worry."

Worry? Who, me? What did he mean, he *had* Aunt Zis? I only thought of little things, like kidnapping and murder.

"I found her wandering around in the parking lot at the mall, Jessie. She was trying to find the bus stop, the one in front of Sears. She was pretty upset."

Considering that Aunt Zis must have used that bus stop a thousand times, I was pretty upset myself when I heard this. "Is she okay?" I asked.

"Sure she is, she's with me. I was going to put her on the bus, but then I said to myself, Victor, stop, think. What if this lady gets lost again, and somebody good like you isn't around? Victor, I said to myself, call her family. Okay, Jessie, I've been calling, and I finally got you."

"I'll come right away," I said, and I was out the door.

In the mall, I found my aunt sitting on a bench next to a small chunky man wearing a plaid jacket. "Oh, here's Jessie," she said. I thought there was a note of disappointment in her voice. No wonder. Victor Perl took her hand and kissed it! "What a lady your aunt is," he said. "We've been having a good talk. Smart lady. She gave me a piece of good advice."

"Just common sense," Aunt Zis said, smoothing down her skirt.

"What happened with the bus stop, Aunt Zis?"

"I don't know," she said. Her hand rose, then fell. "I was going to the bus stop and it was gone. Well, not the bus stop, but how to get there. I just couldn't . . . remember."

Victor Perl took me aside and, in a hoarse whisper, said, "She shouldn't be wandering around on her own, Jessie. Don't get me wrong, but she's old, you have to watch her."

"We do!"

He patted my hand. "I understand, I had a mother. I know what it's like. You have to be extra careful when they get old."

"The experts say we have three kinds of memory," my mother said, climbing a mound of snow on the sidewalk.

"Sure. The things we remember. The things we don't remember. And . . . oh, I know, the things we don't want to remember."

She looked at me and smiled slightly. "Memory for the past, memory for the present, and memory for learned things like riding a bike or swimming. *That* stuff you never forget. It's the day-to-day stuff that goes first. . . . Like the checkbook. Like where the bus stop is. Still, everyone gets lost sometimes. Everyone forgets things. I've gotten lost in that wilderness of a parking lot myself."

"Ma, this is different." I grabbed her arm so she wouldn't slip on the ice. She was just wearing a pair of white sneakers. "She knew there was a bus stop, but how to get there had disappeared completely from her mind.''

My mother sighed and dug her hands into her pockets. ''That man was right, maybe the next time there won't be somebody nice like him around to help her.''

A wind was blowing. We turned up Edgemont Hill, and I pulled my scarf tighter around my neck. ''You know what really scares me, Ma? What else is going to disappear from her mind? What if she went out and forgot our house?''

My mother lit a cigarette, turning her head to blow the smoke away from me. ''So what do we do? Tell her not to go to the mall anymore? I've already taken the checkbook away from her. What's next? She can't go to the drugstore or the market? Why don't we just tell her not to leave the house at all.''

''Don't even say it, Ma. That's awful.''

''I know, Jess! I hate it. She's been independent all her life. I can't do that to her.''

''But we have to make sure she's safe,'' I said. ''There must be something we can do.''

We walked and talked. We went up hills and past all the fancy houses. We talked, but we couldn't come up with any good answers.

THIRTEEN

A Large, Grape-Colored Menu

"I need to get out of my house," Diane said over the phone. "This minute. I can't stand being around my parents. Invite me to sleep over."

"You're invited."

"Ask your mother."

"I don't have to. When are you coming? Do you need a ride? I can ask Ma to pick you up."

"No, meet me at the Grape Kitchen in the mall. I want to eat supper out. My treat."

The waitress at the restaurant decided we were celebrating a birthday. "Our pastry chef will send you a cake for dessert, compliments of." She handed us each a large, grape-colored menu and told us to take our time.

"Order anything you want," Diane said. "In honor of your birthday."

I studied the menu. "Maybe I'll have the stewed lapin. In honor of *your* birthday."

"You like rabbit?"

"So that's what it is. Pass."

"The red snapper with baked mushrooms is good."

"I'm allergic to mushrooms."

"How about calamari? That's what I'm going to order."

"I'm probably allergic to that, too. What is it?"

"Octopus."

"I'm definitely allergic to it."

I settled on pasta primavera, which, at the diner where my mother works, would be called spaghetti and veggies. It was when we were eating dessert that Diane told me her parents were breaking up.

I put down my fork. "No, they aren't."

She bit her lip and sort of shrugged. "Yeah, they are."

"Is that why you were upset last week?"

"Yeah. My mother's flying to Phoenix next week to see my aunt Maxine. She just had a baby, and my mother wants me to go with her. My father's taking my brother and flying to Bethesda to see his sister, my auntie Gracie."

"How many aunts do you have?"

"Seven. Four on my father's side."

"How many cousins?"

"About thirty-five."

"You're lucky."

"Jessie, get a grip. Did you hear what I just said about my parents?"

"Sorry, Diane, sorry."

She picked up the menu and half-smiled. "Jessie, what if you were handed a big purple menu before you were born and told to choose your parents from it? Would you take your same parents?"

"My mother, sure. What about you?"

"I would, too, even though right now I'd like to dump them both. I know why they're doing all this traveling, so they don't have to be with each other. It's like, all of a sudden, after twenty years, they can't even stand being in the same room."

"Are they fighting?"

"You mean arguing and screaming?" She shook her head. "We don't do that in our family. Not the McArdles. It's more like we're walking around inside an ice chest." Her eyes filled, and she pressed the napkin to her face.

The waitress came with the check. I started to take out my wallet, but Diane pushed my hand away. "Just think of it as guilt money, Jessie. My father gave Charlie and me each fifty dollars and said we could do anything we wanted with it."

When we got back to my house, Diane and I couldn't agree on who should take the bed.

"I am not kicking you out of your own bed."

"Diane, you already paid for my meal, that's enough."

"You think that was a sacrifice or something?"

The result was that we both slept on the floor. Two sleeping bags side by side. "This is dumb," I said.

"It sure is," Diane agreed, but neither of us moved.

I was falling asleep when I heard her say, "I never thought anything like this would happen to *me*, Jessie."

My eyes opened. "I know. Your family seemed so happy."

"Maybe my life has been too happy." She ran the zipper of the sleeping bag up and down. "I never had anything really bad happen to me before this. You know what I think? It's my turn now. Everybody has bad stuff, don't they? Why should I be any different? Look at Meadow's little brother, he's got diabetes. My brother, Charlie—"

"What's wrong with Charlie?"

"My mother says he's not having a normal life. He's speeding through school too fast. He's a senior, and he's only fifteen."

"What does Charlie say about your parents?"

"Nothing, he just closes the door to his room." She started crying.

I leaned over and hugged her. "I'm sorry, Diane. I know how much you love your parents."

I kept thinking about Mr. McArdle, what a really nice person he was. No, not nice, *great*. A great father. I couldn't fall back to sleep. I turned one way, then the other. The light from a passing car sprayed the ceiling. Far away, I heard a dog barking. The street was quiet. The house was quiet, my room seemed to breathe in and out. And the same thing happened that had happened in the car.

I felt his presence. I didn't see him, but I felt him looking at me from the darkness. I thought he wanted to tell me something. "What?" I sat up. "*What*?" I leaned forward, trying to see into the shadows, trying to hear, but even as I did, he was slipping away. "Coward," I whispered. "Runaway."

I pulled the sleeping bag up over my ears and turned, looking for a comfortable spot. My hip hurt from the hard floor. I turned again, shifting and turning, turning away from the darkness, from the shadows, from something pressing hard on my heart.

※

FOURTEEN

Jimmy

"There's no James Wells here!"

"Sorry I bothered you." I dialed again.

A sleepy-sounding woman said, "James Wells? Sure. What about him?"

My stomach turned cold. "I'm his daughter, and—"

She gave a high yelp of laughter. "I don't think so!"

"Well, yes. I am, but I haven't seen him since—"

"No, no, no, I don't think so!" She couldn't stop laughing. "James is right here with me. I'm feeding him, as a matter of fact. He loves orange juice in his morning bottle."

"What are you doing, Jessie?" Aunt Zis called upstairs from the kitchen. "Didn't you go to school yet?"

"In a moment. Don't come up, please. I need quiet." My next call—D. K. Wells—was an old man who really wanted to talk and did so. I finally had to hang up on him. Then I got two answering machines, one disconnected number, and one wrong number.

"Jessie, go to school," Aunt Zis called. "You're going to be late."

"Okay, okay." How come she remembered that when she forgot so much else? I dialed quickly. One more call and I'd go. This time a boy—probably about my age, from the sound of his voice—answered.

"Wait a sec," he said. "Dad!" he yelled, "a girl's on the phone for you."

I heard a man saying, "Ask her name."

"What's your name?"

I'd already given it to him once. "Jessie Wells."

"Her name's Jessie Wells!"

"Ask her what she wants."

"What do you want?"

I felt like saying *nothing from you*, but I went through my little speech again. "—trying to find out if anyone in your family knows James Wells," I finished.

"Dad! She wants to talk to you!"

Finally, a man said, "Hello. This is Dennis Wells."

"You don't know me, Mr. Wells, but I called to ask if you're acquainted with James Wells."

"Uh-huh."

"Excuse me? You *are* acquainted with him?"

"Uh-huh."

I was so flustered I began stuttering. "He's, uh, he's, uh, he's my father. So, are you saying—I mean, how do you know him? I mean, are you related to him or what? You both have the same last name," I added stupidly.

"The James Wells I know doesn't live here any-more—is that the one? We're cousins. What do you want to know about him?"

"I was wondering—do you know where he is?"

"No. Not now. What'd you say your name was?"

"Jessie. Jessie Wells. I'm his daughter."

"Oh, yeah. So what's Jimmy up to these days?"

"I don't know, Mr. Wells. I don't know anything about him. That's why I called you."

"Well, Jessie, you didn't call at a good time. I have to go to work. How long are you going to be in town?"

"How long—I'm here. I live here."

"Oh, yeah? Okay, well, nice talking to you. Like I say, I have to go now."

"Wait, wait! Excuse me, do you think we could talk again?"

"Sure. Why not? Give me a call some other time."

"I will," I said. "I'll call you again."

I'd done it. I'd found someone related to James Wells, and it had been so ordinary. No rockets, no gun salutes, no screams. No information, either. Jimmy. Not James. That was my big revelation.

The moon shining into my window woke me. I was thirsty and got out of bed and drank from the faucet in the bathroom. I heard a noise in the front hall. The house was dark but light, full of shadows, everything outlined. I saw Aunt Zis, a blanket wrapped around her shoulders, standing in front of the open front door. Her face was raised, and she seemed to be listening to something.

"Aunt Zis?" I whispered. I was afraid she was sleepwalking; I was afraid to startle her. I saw the moon like a white heart in the sky.

She slowly turned her head and looked at me. "We're living in dangerous times, Jessie," she said.

Cold air flowed over my feet. I put my arm around my aunt and held the small bones tightly. Did she know what she was saying? Was it the bus stop again? Gradually, sounds attached themselves to the still night. Sirens. Dogs. A deep city hum. "Should I close the door now, Aunt Zis?" I said. She was shivering. She let me guide her back to her room.

"Is this an emergency?" Mrs. Kriney, the school secretary, said.

"Well . . . sort of. My aunt's home alone. I want to check up on her. She's old, Mrs. Kriney, eighty-three."

"Don't look at me like it's my fault." She pushed her glasses up on her hair with long red-painted fingernails. "You know the rules, Jessie. Students are not to use office phones except in cases of *genuine* emergency."

"Last week, she got lost in a parking lot."

Mrs. Kriney put on her glasses again to peer at me.

"In the mall." I made a desperate face. "I know it sounds funny, but it isn't, Mrs. Kriney."

If she didn't let me use the phone, I'd run up the street to the variety store, call from the booth there, and if Aunt Zis didn't answer, I'd—well, what would I do? Call the police? And say what? *My aunt was looking at the moon last night, and now I can't stop worrying about her.*

Mrs. Kriney pushed the phone across the counter. "Go ahead."

I gave her a grateful smile and dialed quickly. When Aunt Zis answered, she said, "Where are you, Jessie? Why are you calling home? Aren't you supposed to be in school?"

"I am, Aunt Zis. I was eating lunch, and all of a sudden I had a yen to hear your voice."

"Why in the world?"

"I was thinking about you. I just wanted to know that you were okay."

"What are you talking about, Jessie?"

"Well, since that afternoon you got lost in the parking—"

"Lost?" she interrupted. "I've never been lost in my life."

"Aunt Zis, at the mall. That nice man—Victor Perl—"

"Who?"

"Aunt Zis, you were talking to him. He kissed your hand, he said you were a lovely lady."

"That's quite a story," she said. Her voice trembled. "I don't want to talk about it now." She hung up.

I walked slowly back to the cafeteria. What had I just done? Nothing good. Reassured myself and upset Aunt Zis. When things disappear from your life, whether it's a father or your memory, maybe you don't want to be reminded of it by other people. Maybe you just want to keep it to yourself, and if you can think about it, maybe you want to do that in silence, on your own terms.

FIFTEEN

Red Flags and Green Garbage Bags

"Just by walking a few hours and picking up junk, you can do great things for the environment," I said to my mother. Diane and Meadow had both turned me down already.

"Love to, honestly, sweetie, but my feet..." She pulled into the parking lot where the Save-the-County Walk was starting. A crowd had already gathered, and a woman in a baseball cap was talking through a bullhorn.

I got out of the car, then lingered, leaning into the window. "Ma, if your cousin gets married, what's the person he marries to you?"

"Cousin by marriage."

"What're his kids?"

"Also your cousins."

"Cool. You get more relatives by marriage. Very cool."

My mother laughed. "Depends what kind of relatives they are."

"Yeah. That's true."

When I'd called Dennis Wells again, I got his wife,

who had decided I was selling something. "My husband is a busy man," she said before I could explain, "he's a police sergeant, and he works too hard to be bothered. Let me tell you, you'll be the one who ends up doing the buying. Tickets to the Policemen's Ball."

I watched my mother drive away. I hadn't told her about Dennis Wells yet. So I had a secret, and that was uncomfortable. We'd never had secrets from each other; even when I was little, she told me everything. She would even ask my opinion about changing jobs.

People were milling around, waiting for their team assignment. I was teamed up with a white-haired man with big square teeth, a boy in tiger-striped overalls and a camouflage hat pulled down low, and an older couple wearing identical denim outfits.

"Last year my team tagged twenty-two tires," the white-haired man said. He and the older couple drifted to the other side of the road. That left me and the boy in the camouflage hat.

I started the conversation. "I heard there are two hundred fifty people on this walk today."

He nodded.

"Some people probably think that's a lot." I picked up some slimy plastic. "Two hundred fifty, out of a quarter of a million in the county. That's pretty pathetic. You'd think a few more would want to save it."

He nodded again.

I went into the flattened grass for a beer bottle. There was something gratifying about doing this. It was the same sort of feeling I had when I cleaned my room after a long time of letting it go. I'd throw things out, arrange all my books and stuffed animals, fold every sock, and hang up every pair of jeans.

"I think I might have a vocation for this," I said to the boy. "Seriously, what do you think about me being a sanitation worker?"

He looked at me from under the camouflage cap.

"I'd like driving one of those big rigs. Did you ever see a woman drive one? I haven't. It's about time. Those guys make good money." I must have heard my mother say that a hundred times, and another hundred times that she wished she made even half as much.

"I'd get strong lifting those big cans, and you get plenty of fresh air. How can you beat that?"

He kept staring at me. At first I'd been glad there was someone near my age on the team, but the longer he was silent the more I wished I was on the other side of the road. The adults were talking nonstop.

I decided to be quiet for a while. When I couldn't stand the silence for another moment, I started again. "This is my third year doing this."

"Wow," he managed to say. That was progress.

"And it always rains. Even though the sun is shining now, take my word for it, it's going to rain before the day is over."

"Yeah?"

What a fascinating conversation. "How about you?" I asked.

He sort of jumped. "What about me?"

"How many years have you been going on this walk?"

"First time."

"It's worth it for the T-shirt."

He laughed. It wasn't that funny, but at least he got the joke.

We kept cleaning the roadside. Just as I was ready to break the silence again, he said, "Know what this is?" He held up a big plastic ball with a spout that he'd picked out of the ditch.

"Mutated beach ball," I guessed.

"Party ball."

"What?"

"Beer ball. Holds two gallons." He jiggled it so I

could hear the leftover beer sloshing. He threw it down and flattened it with his heel.

"What's the big deal?"

"They're fun. Instead of a six-pack, you have a party ball."

"I don't admire people getting drunk." He stared at me. "Why do people even drink?" I said. "Don't answer, I know. What's fun about getting wasted, smashed, sloshed, and acting like a fool? My aunt is a strict teetotaler, and so am I." I don't know why I said that. Just to be dramatic, I suppose.

I rolled a tire toward the road and red-flagged it for the truck that would follow us. I felt the boy's eyes on me. He probably thought I was some sort of fanatic.

"One tenth of one percent," he said suddenly.

It was my turn to stare.

"Two hundred fifty people on this walk is one tenth of one percent of the population in the county," he explained.

"You did that in your head? I'm impressed."

"I'm going to be a sanitary engineer. Math is useful."

"Cesspools?"

"Not just cesspools." His face was red.

"Sorry," I said. "Engineering is great. But don't you think structural engineering, bridges and things like that, would be better? Useful *and* beautiful."

We bent down to clean up broken glass. We were nose to nose. "Some eyebrows you have!" he said.

"They're mine."

"I like them."

"You do?"

"Yes."

"Oh," I said. "Okay."

We walked again. "I have this idea," he said, "that the earth is like a house with a lot of rooms."

I looked at him. "How interesting."

"Humans are like the family that lives in the house,

67

but they don't do a good job keeping it clean. Which is bad."

"I know."

I knew something else, too. I was only surprised I hadn't figured it out sooner. But then I'd only seen him once, and he did look different in overalls and a cap than in gym shorts and a sleeveless T-shirt.

"The world as a house," I said. "My language arts teacher would like that analogy."

"Are you going to tell him?"

"Her. Sure. Maybe I'll get extra credit. No, no, no, that wouldn't be honest. It's your idea. Aren't you proud of thinking of such a good idea?" I couldn't resist. "That's so smart of you."

His big face was pinker than ever.

Oh, why torture him? "You know, we've met before," I said. Maybe just a little torture.

"Are you in one of my classes?"

"Wouldn't you remember me if I was, Jack?"

"You know my name!"

I relented. "I saw you at the clubhouse."

"Working out on the machines?" He sounded hopeful.

I raised one of the eyebrows that awed him. "Oh man, watching hunks on machines is not one of my preferred pastimes."

"You're so cute. What's your name?"

"Jessie Wells. Quick, what's yours? Never mind. Just testing." I knotted my plastic bag and dragged it over to the side of the road. "Jack, how'd you get that great idea about the earth being a house?"

"Well, uh, someone told me. My, uh, girlfriend. That is, uh, this girl I talk to on the phone."

I snapped open a fresh plastic bag and, as I did, the truth about Jack Kettle was revealed to me. He was not just a bunch of bulging muscles. He was sweet, smart, and, when put to the test, definitely honest. And then something else occurred to me: I liked him. I liked him a lot.

ll What do you mean, listening to me? Everyone should ...... What do you mean, listening to me? Everyone ...... The sun was streaming out. I filled up a bucket of ....

SIXTEEN

Flecks of Paint

"I don't think Zis has been eating breakfast," my mother said. She picked up her cigarette pack and lighter. "If she gets any skinnier, she'll disappear. Before you go to school, shove some food under her nose and say, *Eat*! And make sure she does, because I can't. When I walk out of here, I can't keep track of who's doing what."

I parked my face guiltily in my cup. I still hadn't told her about Dennis Wells. It was like not telling Meadow about Jack Kettle. I kept thinking I'd get around to it, but half the week had passed, and I hadn't said a word.

"I'll take care of Aunt Zis," I said.

"Thanks, sweetie." She kissed the top of my head.

"Aunt Zis, I put some toast and cottage cheese out on the table for you."

"Why?" She was fastening on a pair of small pearl earrings.

"For your breakfast."

"Do we have strawberries?"

"Just strawberry jam. You have to eat, Aunt Zis. Okay?"

"What do you mean, *I* have to eat? Everyone has to eat."

"You have to eat breakfast is what I mean."

She took off the pearl earrings and put on another pair, tiny gold hoops. "Did you eat breakfast?"

"Yes!"

"What did you eat?" she demanded.

"Cornflakes and milk."

"Good," she said.

While Aunt Zis was eating, I called the Public Safety building. I had never phoned the police before, and when I asked for Sergeant Wells, I had another stab of guilt, as if the cop on the other end of the line knew I was doing things behind my mother's back.

"Hold on," she said.

There was a long silence. Then I heard his voice. "Hello?"

"Sergeant Wells? This is Jessie. Jessie Wells. I called you the other day." He didn't answer. Maybe he didn't remember me. "I'm James Wells's daughter."

"Uh-huh."

"You said we could talk when you had time. So I thought if you told me when that would be—"

"Now," he said.

"Now? Great." I jumped up. I couldn't sit still.

"What do you want to know, Jessie?"

I walked back and forth, pulling the phone cord after me. What did I want to know? "Anything," I blurted. "James Wells is your cousin?"

"Second cousin. Our fathers were first cousins. They had the same grandfather, Hubert Wells, an old farmer."

"Did you and James live near each other?"

"No, no. City boy and country boy."

"He was the city boy?"

"Me! He lived in the country. Hated it. Couldn't wait to get out of Hicksville."

"He lived in a place called Hicksville?"

"No, that's what he called it. He lived in Myrtle."

"Is that up north?" Once, on the way to the St. Lawrence, we had gone off Route 81 there, looking for a bathroom.

"Yeah, cow town. You can smell the manure. Two houses, twenty-five barns, and a bar, that's Myrtle. Jimmy got out of there when he was sixteen."

"Where'd he go?"

"West. Wyoming, I think. What's the cowboy state? Maybe it was Montana. He was back here a few years later, hung around for a while, and took off again. Another two, three years, he comes back for a year or so. Then, what do you know, he's gone again."

That must have been when he left us, I thought. "What was he like?"

"Jimmy? I've been telling you."

He hadn't told me enough. He'd given me two words when I wanted ten . . . ten when I wanted twenty . . . twenty when I wanted a hundred. It was as if he had a painting hidden behind his back and he'd said I could see it, but then he only showed me a measly few flecks of paint scraped from the canvas.

"I mean, what was he like as a person, not just where he lived or went to school."

"What do the kids say today? An attitude. That was Jimmy, he had an attitude. Always wanted you to know he was as good as anybody. Better."

"Was he smart? Was he a good athlete? Was he—"

"Too smart for his own good. The kid had nothing, less than nothing, zero, but he went around like he owned the world."

"He had pride," I said. I had the phone pressed to my ear, trying to absorb everything Dennis Wells was saying. "Do you ever hear from him?"

"I don't hear from my own brother, why would I hear from him? For all I know, he's dead."

"What? I don't think so," I exclaimed.

Death was too passive a state for James Wells. He was the man in motion. Always walking out the door, always leaving, always getting behind the wheel of a car and driving away. James Wells, dead? No, I couldn't believe that.

Just for a moment, though, I pictured him in a grave, hands folded on his chest, clods of earth piled around the deep hole. But when, once more, I tried to see his face, all I saw was darkness.

SEVENTEEN

Things Too Numerous to Mention

After school I walked home with Meadow. It was raining, and I got under her red umbrella with her.

"Is your family project done?" she asked. "I finished mine last night."

"Great." Was this the time to bring up the subject of Jack Kettle? He'd called me the night before and we'd stayed on the phone over an hour. How was I going to explain that to Meadow? "You're doing an oral report?" I asked. My voice struck me as too cheerful. The voice of a hypocrite.

"I'm doing a visual on Thomas Borden Hayes, who was our mayor fifty years ago," Meadow said. "Two buildings, a school, and a street are named after him. I'm related on my father's side. His mother was a Borden. I'm going to use the overhead projector and show old pictures of the city."

"Great."

"My mother took me to the historical society to do my research. I have one picture you're going to love, Jessie, of trolley tracks running down Seneca Street."

"Wonderful."

"What about you? You know, it's due two weeks from Monday."

"Yeah," I said calmly, but my heart took a jump. I stuck my hand out to test the rain. "Nothing to tell, Med. I don't even have an idea yet. Maybe I won't do anything."

"You're going to take a failing mark? Why?"

Good question. Why did I do or not do anything? Why hadn't I worked on the project all these weeks? Why hadn't I told Meadow about Jack Kettle? Were those choices I'd made, or did I just let things happen? The way James Wells must have let things happen. Walking out the door . . . getting in the car . . . driving away . . . So much easier to just keep going, not stop, not think about difficult things.

"I've had a lot of things on my mind. I couldn't concentrate on the project."

"Try harder, Jessie, maybe you'll come up with an excuse Mr. Novak and Mrs. Scher will really like." She stared at me, frowning. I felt that she was looking into my mind, like looking into a smudged window. Any moment now, she'd see Jack Kettle in there.

"I'm worried about you," she said.

"Anyway, I don't like any of my ideas."

"Why don't you interview your aunt Zis?"

"I don't see any buildings or schools that have been named after her."

"She's old, she has a lot of stories, I mean she's like history herself."

It wasn't a bad idea, but if Aunt Zis couldn't remember what happened yesterday, how was she going to remember eighty years ago?

We parted at Ferris Avenue. I called Aunt Zis from an outside phone booth. I'd decided to stop by the diner where my mother worked. Maybe she'd have an idea for me. "Checking in," I said to Aunt Zis.

"Good girl," she said.

"Yeah, I'm good. Are you?" I made her laugh.

The rain was coming down hard and by the time I got to the diner, I was soaked.

"There she is," Randy, the cook, said when I walked in. He was cleaning the grill behind the counter. "How are you, doll?"

"Wet." I hung my jacket on one of the metal trees. Three men were sitting at the counter, leaning over cups of coffee. "Where's my mother?"

"She'll be right out. Take yourself a seat, I'll make you something."

I dried my hair with paper napkins. Randy brought me a plate of toast and a cup of cocoa with whipped cream. "You do toast better than anyone in the entire world," I said, taking a big bite. "Crisp around the edges and soft with melted butter in the middle."

"You're a funny one." He gave my head a swipe with his apron.

I took out my pocket dictionary and started working on an assignment for Mrs. Scher, to look up four words. "With at least two syllables," she'd said, to keep the jokers among us in check. I looked up three D words—duplicity, discretion, and derision. I knew them, but it was interesting to check them out, anyway. Duplicity. Hypocritical cunning or deception. Double-dealing. Related to the word *duplication*.

I had a few uncomfortable thoughts about Jack Kettle and my own duplicity. Or was it discretion? I didn't want to hurt Meadow's feelings. *Sure, Jessie. How about trying again? Maybe you'll come up with an excuse you'll like.*

My fourth word was myrtle. A relief. No guilt associated with that. An aromatic shrub with white, pink, or blue flowers and little berries. That sounded a lot better than "cow town."

"What are you doing?" My mother sat down next to

76

me. "I didn't know you were stopping by. Did you call home?"

"Yeah. She's there. She's fine. I told her I'd be a little late. Ma, I need help with a project that's due next week. You have to give me an idea for it."

"Me, Jess?" Her eyes roamed for customers who might want her. "I have enough trouble getting ideas for myself. When did you get this project? Did the teacher give you enough time on it?"

"Yes, but I've been busy."

"With what? What's more important than school?" She snapped her fingers in my face.

I pushed her hand away. "Don't do that. I've had telephone calls to make."

"Schoolwork first. After that, you talk to friends."

"I wasn't talking to friends, I wouldn't use that as a reason. I was calling those people. The Wellses."

"I thought we agreed you weren't going to do that."

"No, we didn't agree on that, we didn't *agree* on anything. I wanted to call them, and you didn't want me to, but I did. And I found a cousin of James Wells's."

She stood up, then she sat down again.

"His name is Dennis Wells," I said.

"I know," she said.

"What do you mean, you know?"

"I know, Jessie. I know the guy. Dennis Wells."

"You know him? You know he's James Wells's cousin? You told me we didn't have any Wells relatives."

She fussed with the collar of her blouse. It was a pink one she wore only to work. She didn't like the color pink, but all the waitresses had to wear it. "Well, Jess, I thought there was nothing about him that could possibly interest you."

"How would you know that?"

"Judgment call. I make them all the time. That's what being a parent means. Okay?"

"No. I don't like this." My stomach was clenched. "You're always saying I should make up my own mind about stuff." I took a gulp of cocoa. "How can I do that if you keep things from me? What else have you kept from me?"

"Nothing. What is this? What do you want me to tell you? I'll tell you."

"I want to know about my family. I have a right to know about my own family."

"And you do know. Your own family is right here. You, me, and Aunt Zis. That's your family!" She put her hand hard over mine. "Jessie, I never bad-mouthed anyone to you. Did I ever—"

"What are you talking about?"

"I'm trying to tell you something. I'm trying to tell you that there are things you don't know—"

"What things? If I don't know, I want to know."

"Never mind. I don't like to make a fuss about something that's over with."

"What is it I don't know, Maribeth?"

"Too many things, too numerous to mention."

I pulled my hand out from under hers. "Are you talking about James Wells?"

She sat back and folded her arms. "Actually, no. Dennis Wells."

"What about him?"

"Come on, it's the past. Let it be. I didn't tell you some things because I didn't want you to feel bad. If people did things that weren't so great, and if they didn't care about you, I wasn't going to let on to you. What for? Why should a little child be hurt by knowing—"

"I'm not your little child anymore, Ma." I pushed the cup away. "I'm not your adorable puppet."

"Jessie, you are so far from being anyone's puppet—"

"Then just tell me, *what are the things I don't know*?"

She stood up and looked around. "Maybe we should wait until we're home for this."

"You'll forget, or you won't be there, or you'll be too busy."

She bent over, talking into my face, almost whispering. "Okay, listen. When James Wells left, when we needed help, Dennis Wells never stretched out a hand. Not even a finger. He never even called me, not once." Her hand dug into my shoulder. "In some ways, I think that's the worst. Didn't even call and say, 'Maribeth, real sorry about what happened over there, and if I can help you in some way—' "

"Maybe he didn't know."

"He knew. I ran into him one day. You were with me. You wouldn't remember, you were too little. I told him about James Wells and he said he was sorry to hear it. That was it. That was the last I ever heard from him."

I chewed my lip. "Ma. This is the big revelation we had to be home for me to hear? You always say we take care of ourselves, so what difference does it make?"

"You're right, no difference. We did take care of ourselves. We did it! I did it and your aunt did it! No one else. That's my point. We took care of you, we didn't let anything hurt you, we loved you, you were the most important thing in our lives—"

"Ma, you're making speeches."

"Well, I'm sorry, Jessie! I guess you don't understand what a little sympathy would have meant at that moment in my life." I felt the heat of her hand on my shoulder. "I was young. I wasn't even nineteen. Do you know how young that is, Jessie? Sure, I had Aunt Zis. God bless her. *God bless her*! What would I have done without her, but she was already seventy. It was scary. A baby, an old woman, and me."

"But it's okay now, and it happened a long time ago. Can't you forget it?"

"Why should I? I don't carry grudges, but that doesn't mean I don't remember."

"So what are you saying, Ma? You're going to be mad if I go see Dennis Wells?"

"Now you're going to go see him? Why would you want to do that? That man doesn't have a good heart! Haven't I just been telling you—"

"Maybe I'd like to find out for myself, instead of having my life always directed by you."

Her cheeks flared with spots of color. She walked away, to the end of the counter, and began filling sugar jars from a brown bag. I followed her. The sugar flowed into the first jar in a pure white pyramid, and she shook it down and poured in more, then twisted on the metal cap with a harsh grating sound.

Randy, who was working at the grill, tossed a fried egg into the air and slid a slice of toast under it. "How about that, Jessie?" he called.

"The stupid egg trick again?" my mother said.

"Ma. I just want to ask him a few more things about James Wells. Whatever he knows, which I don't think is that much."

"Okay, Jessie, that's cool. Do what you want, just leave me out of it."

"You're not *in* it, Ma."

She looked at me. "That's what you think? I'm not in it? Thank you so much, after all these years." She took the tray of filled sugar jars and walked away.

❀

Station WJES

"Where are you two going, Aaron?" I looked up from the notes I was scribbling on three-by-five cards. It was a rainy Saturday afternoon.

"Movies," Aaron mumbled around his pipe. "You want to come with us, honey?"

"No, she doesn't," my mother said. She was big in a yellow slicker and a floppy rain hat.

"How do you know that?" I said.

She didn't answer me. "Let's go, Aaron." He smiled sorrowfully at me and followed her to the door.

"And good-bye to you, too, lovely person, marvelous human being, Maribeth." The door slammed. I ripped a card in half. *Be calm.* I ripped it in half again. *Come on, you've had fights with her before.*

Yes, but not like this one. This wasn't one of our quickie we-scream-we-shout-we-make-up-with-a-big-hug-and-kiss fights. This had been going on for over a week. Ten days. All I got from my mother these days were cold looks and hard words. And every time we talked, we ended in the same place—my mother wanting one thing and me wanting another, and neither one of us giving an inch.

This wasn't a temporary standoff. It was an impasse, which I understood to mean an impossible place to get by or past or around or through. Like being on a mountain deep in snow and no way over the top. The Donner Pass. Snowed in for the winter, no food, and what was the outcome of that? Cannibalism. The Donner Pass people ate each other. I could see why. My mother and I were already chewing away on each other.

"Aunt Zis, ready?" I said. Out of sheer desperation I'd decided to take Meadow's advice and interview her.

"I've been ready for ten minutes." She was sitting near the window by the dining room table, and in the gray rainy light, with her hands folded in her lap, she looked almost like a girl.

"Let's do a little run-through." I turned on the tape recorder. "Just ignore this. You can pretend I'm Diane Sawyer or Connie Chung. Only a few million people will hear this."

She rapped my hand. "Don't start making jokes. You have to do a good job on this for your class."

"With your help . . ." Was I being too optimistic? I looked at one of my three-by-fives. I had scribbled a dozen questions, but the real question was, what would she remember?

"Okay, here's how it's going to go. I'll start by saying something like, 'Good afternoon, radio audience, this is station WJES, and I'm Jessie Wells, and in our—' "

"Too many *ands*," Aunt Zis interrupted.

I cleared my throat, wondering if it was a bad decision to do this like a radio interview on tape. At least, if I wrote it out, I could fake it a little.

"Jessie! You're dreaming." Aunt Zis gave me another rap on the hand.

"Oh, sorry . . . so then I'll say, 'and in our studio today for our *Interviews with Older People* series is my distinguished guest, blah blah blah, okay, Aunt Zis?

Simple introduction, then I say something about you'll be telling us stories of the past, and off we go. Got it?"

She nodded.

I did my intro, then the first question. "Ms. Young, I believe you went to the inauguration of President Franklin Delano Roosevelt?"

"I did. It was 1933, and I took the train to Washington. There were thousands of people there. They were there for the inauguration, and they were there to demonstrate."

"Why?"

"Why! Don't you know that was the Great Depression? Millions of people were hungry and out of work, and they wanted the president to do something."

"Anything else you want to tell us about that, Ms. Young?"

"Do you have to call me that, Jessie? Call me Aunt Zis."

"This is supposed to be professional. If you went on a radio show, would they call you Aunt Zis?"

"Larry King would."

"When you go on Larry King, you can be Aunt Zis. Ms. Young, would you tell our listeners about growing up in New York City more than eight decades ago?"

"What can I tell you? My family was poor, but we children always had good fresh food."

"What kind of food?"

"Food! My mother made stews. We ate soup. My father took us across the Brooklyn Bridge to get fresh milk. Brooklyn was all farms then. We went out to the barn with the farmer, and she milked the cow for us herself."

Aunt Zis was looking out the window, as if Brooklyn was out there. She started naming all the streets she'd lived on in New York City. "One fifty-nine Orchard Street, Fifteen Grand Avenue, just off the Bowery, Eighty Avenue A, near the river . . ." Then she told how long it took to go by train from Grand Central Station up the Hudson River to Utica, where she had a cousin. She gave the price of bread (five cents a loaf), how much a dozen eggs cost (fifteen cents), and what she'd earned on her first job (thirty-five cents an hour).

Half an hour earlier, she'd been frantically trying to remember where she'd left her house keys. Now she was remembering things from more than half a century ago.

Listening to her tell her stories, I realized that even though she might not remember what day it was, she had so much else stored away in her mind. Things she'd done and seen and thought about. It was as if there was a house she'd once lived in, complete with all its furnishings, rugs, dishes, drapes, and pictures, and no matter where she was, she could walk into the house at any time, touch things, look at them, enjoy them.

I jotted notes for some closing remarks. She started talking about the Great Depression again. "People wrote songs about it. 'Brother, Can You Spare a Dime?' I remember that one. There were soup lines. Some people had nothing, but a lot of people were still okay. I was. I had a job. I remember how guilty I felt every Sunday morning when I treated myself to my favorite breakfast. Pancakes with strawberries, the same thing I wanted that morning your father came back. I'd gone to the market to buy strawberries. By the time I got back, he was gone again."

"James Wells?" I said. "He came here?"

Aunt Zis's soft thin cheeks trembled. "What?"

"You said my father came back here?"

She blinked and pushed the tape recorder away. "You're asking me too many questions."

"Aunt Zis. No more questions. Just answer that one, okay?"

"I'm tired," she said.

"Aunt Zis." I hugged her, and I put my head against her chest the way I used to when I was small. "When

84

did James Wells come back?'' I asked softly.

She didn't answer.

I heard her heart. *Thumpa-a thumpa-a thumpa-a.*
''Why did he come back, why did he do that?''

Thumpa-a thumpa-a thumpa-a . . .

''I need a rest,'' she said. ''Let me go, Jessie. I'm
going upstairs to lie down.''

NINETEEN

In a Heartbeat

When I heard the car door slam, I got up and went out to the hall. It was nearly midnight. I'd been in bed, but not sleeping. Just waiting. My mother looked at me with surprise as she walked in. "You're up late," she said, then she sort of clamped her mouth shut.

"I want to talk to you," I said.

She hung up her yellow raincoat and sat down on the window seat to take off her shoes.

"I want to ask you something. Did James Wells ever come back here?"

She took off one shoe, then the other. "What do you mean, come back?"

"Come back, as in return."

"Who said that?"

"Does it matter? Just answer me, please."

"Did Dennis Wells tell you that?"

"No. Is it true or not, Maribeth?"

"Zis said it, didn't she? Why'd she say that, what did you do to her, Jessie?"

"What did I *do* to her? You think I'd *do* something to Aunt Zis?"

"I don't know, Jessie. Would you?"

My heart beat hard, *thumpa-a thumpa-a*, like Aunt Zis's old heart. I had tumbled so far, from that high place where I was my mother's adored child, who could do nothing wrong, to some other, more desolate spot, a bleak region where nothing I did was right.

I forced myself to speak quietly. I whispered, because what I really wanted to do was scream and lash out at my mother.

"Aunt Zis was upset when she realized what she'd said. She knew you didn't want me to know."

"What did she say, what exactly are we talking about here?"

"She said, *exactly*, that James Wells came back here one day, and she missed seeing him because she was out buying strawberries to put on her pancakes."

"Strawberries?" my mother said, as if I were making it up. She kicked her shoes toward the closet. "I don't remember that."

"But you remember him coming back?"

She shrugged.

"Does that mean yes? When was it?"

"A long time ago."

"How long ago? Last year? The year before?"

"Don't be ridiculous. You were a child. You were barely five years old."

"That's not that young. Why don't I remember seeing him?"

She fumbled around in her pockets for a cigarette.

"Maribeth, no cigarettes! Answer me."

"You don't remember because you didn't see him."

"Wasn't I here?"

"You were here." She started flexing her toes, as if they were tiny fingers she was exercising. "You didn't see him because I didn't want you to."

"You didn't *want* me to. What does that mean?"

"It means, Jessie, that you don't know a thing about your father." Her voice was flat. "It means that I was

87

scared, and I did my best to protect you, because you were what mattered to me in the world. It means I didn't know what to expect of him, and I wasn't going to let him get his hands on you and do one of his good-bye-I'll-be-right-back acts."

"You think he would have *kidnapped* me?"

"Why not? I didn't know what he was capable of. He left us, didn't he? He had no scruples about that. He had no right to come back and torture me."

"Torture you? That's a crazy way to talk. My father came back, and he wanted to see me, and you—" I stopped. My heart was doing that strange old thumping. "Did he want to see me? Is that why he came back?"

"Let's let it go."

"No, let's not!"

"Okay. I don't know the answer to that. He didn't say anything and I didn't give him a chance. You were in the backyard, playing, and I didn't tell him that, and I didn't call you or get you. I told him to leave. That was it." Her face was flushed. "And I'd do the same thing again, in a heartbeat. If you don't understand that, you don't understand much."

"He was my father, I had a right to see him," I said. "That's what I understand. You kept me from seeing him." I stared at her. "I'll never forgive you for that."

TWENTY

Wall of Ice

"My father's moved out," Diane said, practically the moment I walked into her house Sunday afternoon.

"Oh, Diane. That's horrible."

"He's living in the Y downtown. I can't believe he's really gone." Her cheeks quivered. "Now that he's out of the house, my mother's in a much better mood. She's not even sad. She keeps saying it's peaceful now. I feel like I hate her. I don't even want to talk to her."

"My mother and I are fighting, too," I said.

We went into the kitchen and Diane put on a pot of water to heat for spaghetti. I was going to eat supper with her and maybe sleep over. I didn't want to be around my mother. I could have gone to Meadow's, it was closer, but I didn't want to be around her, either. The Jack Kettle thing. My guilty conscience.

"Here, work on this." Diane handed me a grater and a hunk of hard cheese.

"We're going to have tomato sauce, aren't we?" I said.

"Nuh-uh. Olive oil and grated cheese. Don't worry, it'll be good. . . . My aunts from both sides have been burning up the phone wires, trying to get my parents to try again.''

"Diane, that's great."

"No, it's not. I know my parents. If they got together again, it would be, *Let's all pretend nothing happened. Let's all be nice and sweet.*" She dropped a fistful of spaghetti into the boiling water. "They broke my heart, Jessie. They shocked me out of my happy childhood. You can't do that and then act like it's nothing. My aunt Essie says this is the real world, and I'm not tough enough. Maybe, but I say it's my life and I want my parents to respect it, not kick it around like an old shoe."

She looked at me across the counter. "Are you laughing at me?"

"No! No way, Diane. I understand. I always believed my mother respected me. Now I've found out differently. You can't respect someone if you aren't truthful with them, Diane."

I started telling her about James Wells. I was just going to mention him to illustrate what I meant, but the words spilled out. I meant to sketch out the situation, but I ended up saying everything.

We took bowls of spaghetti up to her room and sat on the bed and ate, but I don't know what I ate. I don't know if I ate anything. Something had grabbed me, got hold of me. It was as if now that I'd started, I had to say it all. It was like being on a high-speed train, there was no getting off. At one point, Diane leaned her head on her hand and sort of moaned, "Jessie, oh Jessie." It wasn't pity, I knew it wasn't that. It was a heart cry, as if she knew exactly what I'd felt for so long. The absence, the emptiness, the missing pieces. The space in my life where there should have been a father and wasn't.

"You're the first person I've ever told, Diane." I put my bowl on the floor and lay limply across her bed, my head and arms dangling. I was as tired as if I'd run a marathon.

"You told Meadow," she said.

I shook my head.

She pushed her foot against mine. "If your dad knew you, he'd think you were fabulous."

"And then again, he might just think, Ugh, ugh, who wants an ugly kid like that."

"Your father wouldn't think that. If he saw you, he would just fall in love with you."

I laughed and looked down at the floor. Her rug had a pattern of tiny flowers and leaves. "Oh, sure," I said.

The shadows of leaves dance on the side of the house. The child comes running. The man kneels down. "Is this her?" he says. "Is this my daughter? . . . My god, look at her." He's fallen in love with his child. . . .

Later, when Diane and I were downstairs, cleaning up, my mother called. "Do you want me to come and get you?" she asked.

"No."

"When are you coming home?"

"I'm not sure. Maybe tomorrow, maybe never."

"How're you getting home?"

"If I come, I'll walk."

"I don't want you walking at night."

"Okay! I'll take a bus."

"They're not dependable. I'll be over in an hour. Be ready."

"That's too soon, Maribeth."

"All right, make it an hour and a half." She hung up.

In the car, I could feel my mother's eyes on me. I stared out the window. "Still mad, huh?" she said, as if we'd just had a spat. "What is it that bugs you so much about that business?"

"Are you referring to you not letting me see my father?"

"Right. Would you be a happier person if he had taken a look at you and said, 'So that's the kid. Okay, be seeing you'? Because I'm telling you, that's just what he would have said. If he said anything."

"That's not the point. I could have seen him. My whole life might have been different! It would be something for me to have. Like pride."

"Pride? In him? How about shame?"

"No! Pride! I said what I meant, Maribeth! You, you work, you work three jobs, you do too much, I'm full of pride for you, sometimes I feel like it chokes me, because I don't do enough back for you—"

"Come on, that's not right—"

"—and him, I have nothing," I said, talking over her. "No pride, no shame, nothing." My eyes smarted. "I want something, I want to know about him. The truth. Not those baby stories you've been telling me all my life. *Story of my life*," I mimicked.

She pulled the car over to the curb and stamped on the brake, jolting me forward. "James Wells? You couldn't *know* him, Jessie, not the way you're talking, not if you sat and stayed with him for a hundred years. He didn't give himself to anyone, he wouldn't tell you anything. Everything bottled up, and you never knew why he was charming you or why he was mad or why he was anything. You don't know what it's like, living with someone like that. Guess why I make so much noise sometimes, why I love to hear you do the same? Because I lived with a man who was like a blocked-up sewer."

"I don't want to hear this," I said. For years it had been the prince with his leather jackets and beautiful car, and now it was *sewers*?

"No, you're going to hear it," she said. "You want the truth, and I'm going to give it to you. I begged him

92

to talk to me, to tell me how he felt, tell me what was bothering him. You think I didn't try? I tried. Let me help you, let me make you happy, just open up a little. That's all I'm asking. No. Nobody allowed in. He talked or he didn't talk, on his terms. Everything on his terms. He snarled or he smiled, and I never knew the why for anything. Nothing I did suited him. I didn't know how to cook, I didn't know how to dress, I didn't know how to talk to people, I didn't even know how to take care of you.''

We were sitting side by side, but there was a wall between us. Rock and ice. She was on one side, I was on the other. I could barely hear her. I could hardly make out what her words meant.

''Sometimes he left for hours and then came back. Twice he left for days, and I thought he was gone for good, and then he came back and sat there and stared at me and didn't say a word.

''I was in terror. And I had no words for it. Nobody said things like emotional abuse in those days. I never knew what was going to happen. And then one morning he looked at his watch and said he would go out for a while, and when I asked him where he was going, he said, 'Nowhere,' and that was where he went.

''Nowhere. Nowhere I knew about. Nowhere near us, ever again. Why did he leave? Who knows? All I know now is that it's the best thing he ever did for me. I cried my heart out for three weeks, and then, when I knew he wasn't coming back, this time or ever . . .''

''Three weeks?'' My mind fastened on that detail. ''You cried for three weeks? Why did you lie to me? You always said three days.''

''Why do you call everything I do a lie? Why should I tell a little child that for a while her mother thought she was going to die of a broken heart? What would be the point? You were my life, you were what mattered,

93

and I would have seen him in hell before I let him anywhere near you, even for a second.''

She stuck a cigarette in her mouth and said, ''Now
tell me I was wrong. Go ahead. Tell me.''

TWENTY-ONE

This Is the Air He Breathed

When I saw Jack Kettle waiting for me on the top step of the library, I almost walked away. I could have. He was looking in the other direction, and he didn't see me right away. Then he turned and came bounding down the steps. "Hi!"

"Hi," I said. "I see you've changed your headgear." He was wearing a black cowboy hat.

"Did you have trouble recognizing me?" His face got pink.

"I'd know you anywhere."

He pushed the cowboy hat back on his head. "Aw, shucks."

After that great beginning, neither of us said a word. It was embarrassing. Me, who always knew how to talk, suddenly didn't—because what flashed into my mind was, *This isn't just meeting downtown, it's a date. What am I doing?*

Some girls sat down on the steps behind us and began arguing in loud voices. Jack crossed his arms, then uncrossed them, and I crossed mine. *Say something,* I ordered myself. I lifted the hair off my neck and got out, "Hot for April."

95

"Yeah," he said.

"Last year it snowed on this date."

"Wow."

"Two inches."

"No kidding."

"But it melted fast."

"That's good."

It was? I decided I'd cut my tongue out before I said one more word about the weather. "Were you waiting for me very long?"

"No. Well, yeah."

"The bus was sort of slow. Sorry."

"No prob. What do you want to do?"

"What do *you* want to do?"

"Anything you want to do."

"How about a bus ride?"

He looked surprised. "Okay with me," he said.

"Not just anywhere," I said. "I want to go to Myrtle."

"What's that?"

"Little town north of here."

"Myrtle. Want to tell me why?"

I nodded. "But not right now."

"Ladies and gentlemen," the bus driver said, "there is no smoking on this vehicle. Please be courteous to your fellow passengers, relax, and enjoy the ride."

Jack had a pocket chess set with him. He put it on the seat between us and taught me the basics of the game.

Every five minutes, the bus stopped at another tiny place. The stop for Myrtle was in front of a grocery store with two gas pumps. There was a row of houses strung along the road. On the other side of the street were a few more houses, a laundromat, and a feed store with a faded sign flapping in the wind. The air smelled the way Dennis Wells had said it would, like a barn.

"What now?" Jack said.

"I want to walk around and look at things." I still hadn't explained myself, why we were here. We walked to the corner. The houses were all small and plain. Washing was hanging on lines strung across porches. Pickup trucks in every yard. Not too far away, I heard the clank of farm machinery.

This is where James Wells lived, I told myself. This is the air he breathed. We passed a tiny park. A metal sign said this was the site of an ancient Oneida Indian village. I wondered how many times James Wells had read this sign. At the edge of town, we saw brown fields and ditches half-filled with snow. The barn smell was everywhere. *These are the things he saw, the sounds he heard, the smells he smelled.*

"So this is Myrtle," Jack said.

"Are you sorry you came?"

"No. It's an adventure. Jack and Jessie's exciting adventure." Suddenly he had his arms around me, a big bear hug.

"Give me air," I said. I wanted to push him away and I wanted to pull him back. We started walking again, holding hands. He had a big hand.

A woman pushing a stroller with a little boy in it stared at me. "Excuse me. Do you know me?" I said. "Do I look like someone you know?"

"What?"

Jack stared at me, too.

The woman bent over the stroller and adjusted the little boy's tiny baseball cap, then patted him all over, as if she were afraid parts of him were missing.

"Sorry. I'm not making sense. Do you know the Wells family? James Wells? He lived here. I look sort of like him, and I thought maybe you recognized me."

She straightened up. "I just moved here a few years ago, I'm practically a stranger myself." She walked away.

"Who's James Wells?" Jack said.

We sat down on a railing near an empty building, and for the second time, I told someone about James Wells. It wasn't like telling Diane. Same words, same feelings for me, but it was the difference between going into a room alone and going in with someone you know. Diane had been by my side while I talked. I couldn't tell where Jack was—he could have been here, or he could have been fifty miles away. He just sat there, looking down at the dirt and sometimes nodding his head.

When I was finished, he said, "Some story."

"It's not a story. It's the truth."

"Oh, I know that." He patted my hand.

"I shouldn't have dragged you here," I said. "It wasn't fair of me. It's not your business—"

"You didn't drag me. Anyway, I'm glad I'm here. I mean, I am if you are."

We sat there for a few more minutes. "So you're just planning on going around, sort of talking to people and seeing what you can find out?" Jack said.

"More or less." I went into the grocery store and asked to use the phone book. There wasn't a single Wells in it, and the woman behind the counter said she'd never heard of James Wells.

"I know James Fortune." She wore glasses with bright orange frames.

"Wells," I repeated. "He used to live here."

The door chimes sounded. A man in green work clothes bought a carton of cigarettes. "You ever know anybody named James Wells?" she asked him. He fingered the stubble on his cheeks, then shook his head. Jack bought chips and soda. A girl came in, but she looked too young to even ask.

"What if nobody knows him?" I said.

"You haven't asked around that much yet." Jack gave my hand a squeeze.

On a side street, a woman was hanging up wash in a yard. I talked to her over the wire fence. She squinted at me and said, "I might remember a James Wells." About a dozen little kids were running around in the yard. She took the clothespins out of her mouth. "If he's the one I'm thinking about, if he's that one, he was on the wrestling team in junior high school. Was he a wrestler?"

"I don't know. What did he look like? Did he have eyebrows like mine?" It sounded ridiculous.

"How old would he be?" she asked.

"About thirty-six," I said.

"Thirty-six? That sounds right. That's how old I am." She gestured to the kids. "You don't think those are all mine, do you?"

"This is preschool?" Jack asked. "My older sister does that in her home."

"Amanda," the woman called to one of the little girls, "don't you do that to Kevin, or you'll have to go inside."

"Do you remember anything else about James Wells?" I asked her.

She snapped a sheet and pinned it to the clothesline. "My girlfriend liked him, that's why I remember him at all. I wasn't interested in wrestling, but a couple times we went to watch Jimmy. That's what she called him."

"Yes!" I gripped the fence. "That was his nickname."

"My girlfriend told me he was a foster kid, lived around with a bunch of different people. She had such a crush on him. He never talked to her, never talked to anyone if you ask me, but she almost died every time she saw him—Amanda," she yelled again. "You leave Kevin alone."

"Does your girlfriend still live here? Do you think I could speak to her?"

"I wish you could. I wish *I* could! She was the best friend I ever had. She was living in Thailand last time I heard from her. She married an English guy, I don't know what he does, but she's around the world—Amanda!" She took off after the terrible Amanda. "That's all I know, anyway," she yelled back to me.

We walked again. Everywhere we went I thought of James Wells. Had he stood on this street? Had he lived in this house? Had he had friends in that house?

At a corner, there was a small cinder-block building. The sign said ICE CREAM HOMEMADE. "My treat," Jack said, opening the door.

"No, mine," I said.

"Jessie—" He got that pink look again. "You're a girl."

"Jack. Surprise, I know it."

Inside, an old man sat on a box, bent over and staring down at the floor. "Can we get some ice cream?" I said.

"Ay-uh." The old man got up from the box. He was permanently bent over, like an upside down L, his back nearly parallel with the floor. He went behind the counter. "I got vanilla and I got chocolate."

"Vanilla for us both," Jack ordered.

"I'm trying to find out about someone named James Wells," I said to the old man's bent back. "Maybe you can help me. He's my father, and he used to live here in Myrtle."

He dipped the ice cream. It took him a long time.

"I talked to somebody who thought he was on the school wrestling team," I said.

He tilted his head up toward me. "Oh, ay-uh, I know."

"You knew James Wells?"

"Ay-uh, I sure did. Wrestling team, uh-huh. Strong boy. He always came in for ice cream. He liked my ice cream. He liked the raspberry best."

"That's my favorite flavor!" I looked at Jack. "No kidding, I always get raspberry."

The old man handed us our cones, then shuffled over

to the box and sat down again. "The family used to live out back behind the Hudlen place."

"The Hudlen place?" I said. "Where's that?"

"Gone now. Hudlens are all gone. Like the Wellses. Farm's all gone. Land was sold to some city people. Back then, the Hudlens lived in the house and the Wellses lived out in the trailer. He was the help, you know, the hired hand."

"James? He was the hired man?"

"His father. Rawson, his name was. And Janice, that was her name."

My grandparents. I leaned against the wall, watching the ice cream soften in the cone. How strange that I had never thought about James's parents before. It was as if I'd been looking through a slit in a wall and believed I was looking through a window. I had thought only about *him*, James Wells, as if he were an actor stepping onto a bare stage to perform in the story of my life. As if his story—like my mother's, like Aunt Zis's, like my own— wasn't knotted up into so many other stories.

The old man looked up at me. "They never was steady. Too much drinking, both of them. When the man drinks, it's bad, but when a woman drinks—" He spit into a can next to the box. "Pitiful people. The boy had to go live with other folks. They locked him out one time. He was ten, eleven. Strong little boy, though."

"I heard that he left Myrtle when he was sixteen," I said.

"Doesn't surprise me a bit."

"Is there anything else you can tell me about him?"

"Told you what I know."

"Thank you. Could I come see you again sometime?"

"It's a free country."

We went out. "Your ice cream," Jack said.

It was melting. I handed it to him to eat. I was numb. My whole face was as numb as if someone had hit me. Always before, I had thought this way about James

101

Wells: He left me, he disappeared without a trace. Now it came to me that it wasn't the whole truth. He had left me his eyebrows . . . his voice . . . a taste for raspberry ice cream . . . Little things, but there they were. And here I was—the trace of him in the world.

We went back to the grocery store to wait for the bus. Lights were coming on in the houses. I stood on the concrete apron near the gas pumps. "Well, I found out some things," I said.

Jack stood next to me. "Did you find what you wanted?"

"Yes and no. I still don't know why he left us." The wind was blowing and there was a chill in the air. "I don't know why he never cared about me."

Jack took off his jacket and put it around my shoulders.

"Just let me warm up, then I'll give it back," I said.

"No, you keep it." He put his arm around me, and then he kissed me. I closed my eyes and thought, *Jessie, kiss him back.* But really I didn't have to tell myself anything. I was doing it as I thought it.

On the bus, Jack and I held hands. We sat close, and he dozed off. I was warm inside his jacket, half-sleepy myself, but thinking about James Wells.

Once there'd been a prince in a leather jacket . . . and a man who wanted a home, a big house . . . and a man who made my mother cry. But before all that, there'd been someone else, too. A boy living with his parents in a trailer . . . a boy who didn't talk much . . . a boy locked out of his home . . . a boy who had to live with other people. I felt so sorry for that boy.

TWENTY-TWO

Little Pearls

"Myrtle," my mother said, for about the tenth time. And Aunt Zis chimed in, "You went to Myrtle? Why did you do that?"

"Coming home at eleven o'clock at night?" my mother went on. "You didn't tell anyone where you were going! Myrtle," she said again, as if she hated the taste of the word in her mouth. "Did you like it?"

"Not particularly." We were in her bedroom. She was in bed, Aunt Zis was sitting on the edge of the bed near her, and I was standing in the doorway—hovering there, just waiting for her to have her say and release me.

"Your aunt was frantic," she said. "We couldn't imagine where you were. If you didn't think about *me*, at least Zis. You scared the life out of her. We called your friends, we called Meadow, we called Diane, no one knew anything."

"All right, you said that already. Aunt Zis, you should go to bed," I said. "You look exhausted."

"I am. I'm very tired." She held her robe close around her. As she left, I whispered, "I'm sorry, Auntie."

She patted my arm and went on down the hall to her room.

"Why didn't you at least call?" my mother said.

"I didn't think of it."

"You didn't think of it. Is that supposed to be an apology or an excuse?"

"Neither!"

My mother twisted the sheet as if it were a chicken whose neck she'd like to wring. Me. My neck.

"What is happening to you? I don't recognize my daughter standing there, she's like a heartless stranger."

My legs felt leaden, too tired to hold me up. My eyes wanted to close. Why *hadn't* I called? I'd never thought of it, not once, never thought of my mother or Aunt Zis, only of myself and what I wanted.

"I didn't mean to upset Aunt Zis. I'm sorry."

"Sorry is not enough." My mother's voice rose. "Do you have any idea how *I* felt when I got home and found out you'd been missing for hours? Do you know what I thought? I thought you were gone. I thought I'd never see you again."

"Don't be crazy," I said.

"No, it's not crazy . . . it's happened before." She was crying, deep shuddering sobs. It was more awful than if she had leaped up and hit me in the face. Her crying petrified me. I had never seen her like this.

All my life, in the story I knew so well, I had heard her say, *I cried for three days.* . . . It had never seemed an awful thing to me. I had loved those words, they were familiar, they were part of the story. I'd imagined her tears like little pearls decorating her face. I'd imagined her, after three days, springing from the couch and going off to work like one of the seven dwarfs, singing and merry.

"I can't stand it," she sobbed. "You've changed so much. I don't know you anymore. You're breaking my heart."

I told myself to go to her, but something held me where I was. I wanted to do it—go and put my arms around her, the way I'd done so many times before. But I didn't. I couldn't. I couldn't move.

TWENTY-THREE

A Bizarre Layer Cake

In some ways, the next day was the strangest or maybe just the most intense day I'd ever lived through. I woke up early, with the alarm clock, because I had a seven o'clock dentist appointment. Although usually I really hate going to the dentist, I was so happy thinking about Jack that I didn't even care. That was the good stuff, and it lasted about one minute. Then my aunt came into my room. Crept in, is more like it. She was holding her back, making little moaning sounds with every step.

"What's the matter?" I said, alarmed.

"I could hardly sleep last night thinking about you and your mother." Her cheeks were deeply creased, and her eyes had that dim, cloudy look they got when she was agitated.

She sat down on the side of my bed and took my hand. "Jessie. I know I'm old. I know I forget things. But there are some things I know and you don't. You should know that your mother hasn't had an easy life. And she doesn't deserve to be treated the way you're treating her."

"Aunt Zis, stop." I threw off the covers. "I don't want to hear this, please! I didn't go to Myrtle to upset you or Ma. I'm not doing anything because I mean to ups—''

"You don't know what it means," she went on. "You're still young, you don't know how people suffer." She was trembling, her hands and her arms were trembling slightly and constantly. "You shouldn't be making it harder for your mother. That's not right."

My throat was tight. I wanted to tell her she wasn't being fair. I wanted to ask why she was taking my mother's side against me. I wanted to defend myself, and I wanted to throw myself into her arms for the love and approval she'd always given me.

All day long, not one thing went the way I thought it would. Every moment brought another mood. I was depressed, sad, hopeful, anxious, ecstatic, self-reproachful, and even, at moments, thinking about Jack, happy again. If the day had been a cake, it would have been a layer cake—a bizarre layer cake with sweet parts and poison parts.

My appointment with the dentist, for instance, ended with my running out of the office, my cavity unfilled, my jaw swollen with Novocain, and everyone calling my name.

While I was sitting in the chair, waiting for the shot to take effect, I read a magazine story about a girl who had cancer. The night she was dying, she wanted her mother with her, but she begged the nurses not to call too soon. "My mom needs her sleep."

I read that as if it had been written expressly to reproach me for my selfishness, to point out how I not only didn't think of my mother before myself, but I cruelly tormented her. I yanked off the pink paper bib. Then I was down the hall and out of the office with people calling after me, "Jessie! What's the matter?"

Why do people always ask that question? *What's the matter*? As if, when you do something impulsive, you could calmly list the reasons. Impulsive means that you don't know your reasons, or if you do, you don't care! Not at that moment. All you know and all you care about is what you're feeling, and what you're feeling is the impulse.

One thing that was not impulsive was my decision to talk to Meadow. I caught up with her in the hall, between classes.

"Hi," she said. "Where were you yesterday? Your mother called three times to see if you were at my house!"

"I know. I have to talk to you, Med."

"You sound grim."

"No, just my stomach's sort of queasy." I almost felt nauseated. I'd made up my mind to tell her about Jack before I got in any deeper. Maybe not all and everything—I couldn't exactly see myself reporting the kiss—but *something*.

"You're sick?" She put her arm around me. "You want to go to the nurse? I'll go with you."

She was so sweet I lost my nerve. I caved in and didn't even mention Jack. Instead, I told her about James Wells. Which was something else I'd neglected to do. We walked up the stairs together. We didn't have much time before the bell, but I managed a kind of condensed version of the story.

"I can't believe I never knew any of that," she said. "I always thought your parents were, well, divorced or separated."

"They are," I said.

"You know what I mean, sort of more normal." She hit herself on the forehead.

"Don't worry about it, Med. I never wanted to talk about it."

The bell rang then, and it saved me from making another big mistake. I'd been on the point of blurting out that she wasn't the first person I'd told this story to.

108

Great. My best friend, and she's the last to know. Maybe I could set up shop in how to hurt everybody's feelings.

That afternoon, I finished off my wonderful day with my family history report. Several people presented theirs before me. Kevin Mock brought in a turntable and played songs from Greece. They were on old 78 RPM records, and even Mr. Novak got excited about that. "Those are classics!" he said.

Heather Lo had a decorated vase that her great-grandmother had brought with her from China. She told a family story about her great-grandmother's sister who had drowned in a well when she was a teenager. "It was called an accident," Heather said, "but there's a good chance that she committed suicide. The family was poor, and they had arranged to marry her off to someone old, who would give them money for her. Females have never been valued as much as males in that society."

"Dynamite stuff, Heather," Mr. Novak said. "Jessie?"

I put the tape deck on his desk and turned it on. Mistake number one. I should have introduced what I was doing. Mistake number two—my editing. The first thing I heard was Aunt Zis saying, "Don't start making jokes."

I reached over and turned off the tape. "Sorry. What you're going to hear is in the form of a radio interview." I gave some background about Aunt Zis and started again.

Meadow called me later to find out how it had gone. "Not too bad," I said, and I told her some of the things I'd said at the end. "I said it was amazing to think that Aunt Zis was born at a time when telephones were still considered a wild innovation, and today she reads and watches everything she can about the space program. Mr. Novak liked that."

"You'll probably get a better mark than I will. Anything else you want to tell me?"

"No!" I said, but of course there was. Jack Kettle.

TWENTY-FOUR

Disobedience, Disorder, and Defiance

A patrol car was parked in front of school, with a cop standing beside it. He was talking to Peter Krill, a boy I knew from math class. Peter pointed to me, and the cop nodded.

For one blindingly weird moment, I thought my mother had called the police to arrest me. The charge was clear—disobedience, disorder, and defiance. And while she was at it, she could add deceit. Welcome once more to the D zone.

I walked slowly over to the patrol car.

"You Jessie?" the cop asked. "I'm Sergeant Wells. Dennis Wells."

"Hello!" I wanted to shake, but he kept his hand resting on the baton hooked to his belt. Such a cop thing to do. And he looked like my idea of a cop—big, balding, and overweight. His eyes surprised me, though, large and dark, with long lashes. Pretty eyes, like the eyes of one of the horses at the stable.

He studied me. "Yeah. You look like Jimmy," he said.

"The eyebrows," I said.

He nodded. "What are you, Jessie, sixteen, seventeen?"

"I'll be fifteen next month. I'm big for my age."

"You didn't get that from Jimmy. Short little guy."

"I know, my mother told me."

"What's her name again?"

"Maribeth. She said she met you."

"Yeah? Maybe with Jimmy."

"And me," I said. "When I was a baby."

"I don't remember. Could be. I got something for you, Jessie." He took an envelope from his pocket.

Inside was a snapshot of a boy standing on the steps of a house. "Who is it?" I asked, but I think I knew right away.

Heat ran through my hands straight up into my eyes, turning them hot, almost gluey. It was the first picture I'd ever seen of James Wells.

I smoothed out the photo. I almost didn't want to look at it. I'd tried to imagine his face so many times, and every time it had been shadowy, hidden. I checked out what he was wearing—chinos and a plaid shirt. I looked at the house with its peaked roof, and the porch, and the two tubular metal chairs on the porch. I saw the tree by the side of the house, and I saw that it was a summer photo.

And finally I looked at him. His shirt was open at the neck . . . hair blowing across his forehead . . . a little smile.

I put the picture carefully back in the envelope and held it out to Dennis Wells. "Thank you for showing it to me."

"Keep it," he said.

"Keep it?"

"It's no use to me." He got in the patrol car and turned on the ignition.

111

I bent down to the open window. "Well, thank you. Thank you, Sergeant Wells."

"You don't have to call me Sergeant, you know." He gunned the engine. He looked faintly disgusted. "What's wrong with Dennis? I thought we were cousins."

I stuck the picture in the frame of my mirror, opposite the ones of Aunt Zis and my mother. I spent a lot of time looking at it. Every morning, while I was dressing, I studied it, and every night, before I went to bed. Who had taken the picture? Maybe someone he was living with—a friend or a foster parent. Maybe a girlfriend. James. Jimmy. My father. I thought he was so handsome, so attractive. A hero! He must have been wonderful. Smart and good-looking. I loved his smile. For about two days, I was in love with him.

Then I became unsure. I began to see other things, that he looked a little superior and a little scared and a little flashy, too, all of it, all at once. There was more than one boy hidden there. Up front was the kind of boy who would always have a girlfriend. A mantelpiece boy—almost too good-looking, the kind of boy who needs girls hanging around, admiring him.

I saw more. I saw the way he stood on the porch step, ready to leap off, leap away. Get away. And I saw the way his smile was saying *I'm leaving . . . see you around. . . .* And then there were his eyes.

I couldn't see his eyes. He hadn't looked into the camera. No matter how I turned the photo, I could never get those eyes to meet mine.

TWENTY-FIVE

Monkey Bars

"You guys stay nearby," I called to Rudy and Kim, the kids I was baby-sitting. Meadow and Diane had come with me to the playground, and we were all sitting on top of a picnic table.

Kim turned and waved. "We're going on the monkey bars." She was five and Rudy was four. They were best friends.

"Don't get out of my sight," I warned. "Either of you. Hear me?"

"They're practically under your nose, Jessie," Meadow said. "Leave them alone. You're a nervous wreck with them."

"I was only supposed to baby-sit Rudy," I said, talking fast. I *was* nervous. "When I got over to Professor Berman's house, Kim was there, too." I glanced at the kids again, then unzipped my knapsack and took out the bus schedule I'd picked up in the station.

"What's that?" Meadow said.

"Look, see the name of this town?" I pointed. "This is where James Wells grew up. Myrtle. I went there last Sunday. I went up by bus."

Meadow's hair was in two long braids, and her face

stood out sharply between them. She looked at me as if she knew what I was leading up to. "You went alone?"

"No." I was sweating. I lifted my shirt and fanned my belly. "Med, there's something . . . something I've been wanting to tell you. Sort of a confession." I wished I hadn't used that word. "I went to Myrtle with Jack Kettle."

She looked at me in a stupefied way. "That doesn't make sense. You don't even know him."

"He was on the Save-the-County Walk."

"That was weeks ago," she said. "You've known him all this time and never said a word to me?"

"I meant to, Med. I was going to. He was on my team, we were together the whole day, then he called me once or twice, and we talked. You know." I was chattering. "You were right, Meadow, he is nice."

"Don't tell me that! Not now! I always thought if I could trust anyone in the world, it was you," she said.

"You can!"

"Oh no, oh no!"

"Meadow, I'm upset about this, too."

"Shut up, don't you dare say that to me! Why did you to go to Mirrle with him?"

"Myrtle," I said. "I wanted to see where my father grew up, and Jack had called—" I coughed hard. "So, anyway, we met downtown and he just sort of ended up going with me."

"*Just sort of*? You're lying, Jessie. I know your face. I know you. Look at her, Diane, her face is all red and slimy-looking."

"Come on, you two, don't fight," Diane said. "Talk about it, you don't have to fight."

"What else, Jessie?" Meadow said. She had a little knife face. "There's more, isn't there?"

I pulled at a weed that had grown up through the picnic table. "No," I said, and then suddenly—I don't know why I did it—I said, "He kissed me."

Meadow leaped off the table as if she'd been burned. "You're not a friend," she shouted. "You are dirt!" She ran over to the monkey bars and swung herself off the ground. I sat still, pulling at the weeds. "Go talk to her," Diane said.

I brushed myself off and went over to Meadow.

"Go away," she said, swinging her feet toward my face. "Get away from me. I'll bite you!"

"Med, I swear I would never have let it happen on purpose. I wouldn't hurt you like that—"

"I don't want to hear it." She dropped down from the monkey bars and walked away.

TWENTY-SIX

A Storm

I waited for my mother to mention the picture. I waited for an explosion, I waited for her to do something in her dramatic fashion—tear the picture off the mirror, scatter the pieces over the floor. I imagined her carrying on about my disloyalty, and my coming right back at her, *That was mine! You have no right to destroy what's mine.*

Satisfying. But even more satisfying was imagining saying coolly, as if I were a guide at a museum pointing out the facts, *I'm clarifying my thoughts about James Wells and about myself, and us. The photograph is an essential clue to my life. I'm not just your daughter, I'm the daughter of both of you. I am him in some ways, and you in some ways, but most of all I am myself. And although this may surprise you, that means I don't always want what you want.*

These words thrilled me, and I waited for the moment when I could say them to her. But we weren't talking. We weren't even screaming at each other. *That* would have been normal, friendly, even.

One evening, out of the blue, she said, "I suppose you're going through a teenage identity crisis."

"*What*?"

She stuck a dry cigarette in her mouth. "That's what Aaron says. He says it's hard being a teenager."

"I don't want you talking about me to other people."

"Aaron's not other people."

"Just don't talk about me, even to Aaron. And I'm not a *teenager*, I'm a person. And another thing—I'm not having a crisis, you are."

The cigarette wobbled on her lip. "You've changed, you're doing things . . . you're obsessed. Don't think I'm not aware, I haven't given up being your mother. I know what's going on. Where did the picture come from? Did it come from him?"

"What him? You mean James Wells?" I laughed and went downstairs. It was getting dark outside. Thunder rumbled in the distance. I turned on lights.

My mother followed me, turning them off. "Who gave you the picture?" she said.

"Not James Wells."

"Who?"

"Dennis gave it to me."

"*Dennis*?"

"My cousin Dennis." I stood at the sink and looked out at the darkening sky. "Did you ever see that picture of James Wells before? You had other pictures, didn't you? Did it make a big pile when you threw them out? You did, didn't you, throw out everything of James Wells's? You cleaned him out of the house, so I wouldn't have anything." My throat tightened, but I kept my voice even. "You missed one thing." I took his buckle out of my jeans, where I'd taken to carrying it.

She examined it for a moment, then shrugged and gave it back to me.

"He was good-looking," I said. "I can see why you—"

"His looks were not *why* anything," she interrupted. "I fell in love. I thought he was good, and smart, too.

That was what I wanted, a good father for my child, someone smart enough not to take a boat out in a storm without wearing a life jacket.''

"I feel sorry for him," I said. "For his life. He had a tough time in life."

"So do a lot of us, Jessie, but that doesn't mean we run out on people."

"Well, I can't hate him," I said. "I just can't!"

She tore lettuce into the colander. "Do you honestly think I wanted you to hate him? If I wanted that, I could have made damn sure of it."

"Maybe you didn't want me to hate him," I said in a moment, "but you didn't want him to be real to me, either."

"Now what does that mean?"

"That means all the phony stories you told me." I opened a jar of tomato sauce and dumped it in a pot. "His BMW, his leather jacket, his—"

"All right, all right," she said.

"—and all the things you didn't tell me, like his horrible life and his horrible parents."

"Jessie, what do you want me to say? Everything's a problem for you these days. Yes, I knew about his parents. No, I didn't want to tell you." She sliced carrots with hard strokes. "One, I don't think it's any excuse for the way he acted. And two, I don't happen to think a parent has to tell a child every bad thing in the world. We've talked about this before."

"I'm not a child. When are you going to understand? I deserve the truth, whatever it is. It's my life, too. Why can't you understand that?" I turned away, so I wouldn't cry.

Suddenly the storm came. There was thunder over the house. The windows rattled. "I better go check on Zis," my mother said. My aunt hated storms. They frightened her.

"Yes," I managed to say. "Good idea."

She started out, then said, "I do understand. I'm trying to, anyway, Jessie."

I stayed in the kitchen, getting things ready for supper. After the storm passed, we all sat down to eat.

TWENTY-SEVEN

Scared to Death

My mother came in from work, stuck her head in the door of my room, and said, "Jessie, you want to listen to something?"

"What?" I was at my desk, doing homework. I put my finger in my book and waited. Things were still pretty stiff between us.

"You're not going to believe this," she said. "I'm having trouble believing it myself." Then I thought I heard her say, "James Wells." She went into a spasm of coughing and couldn't speak for a minute.

"Yeah, Ma, just keep smoking," I said.

Her face was red. Still coughing, she said, "I saw him. He's here."

I was calm and thought, *She doesn't mean it. This only happens in movies. The Big Scene. Lots of soppy music, long-lost dad walks in the door. Get out the tissues.*

"He came into the diner for dinner," my mother said. She was still standing in the doorway. "He sat down in a booth, picked up a menu, just like any customer. He was on Victoria's station, I had the one in back. I thought, *It's not him, my eyes are playing a trick on me.* I went over to Victoria and said, 'See that guy? I think

120

it might be my ex.' She said, 'What do you mean, you *think*, don't you know your own ex?' I said, 'It's been a while, Victoria.' She said, 'You want me to dump his dinner in his lap?' ''

"What'd you do?"

"I wasn't going to do anything. I didn't want to talk to him. But then—" She shrugged and leaned a little deeper into the room. "I thought you'd want me to say hello to him, at least."

I looked up. "Is that what you really thought?"

She nodded. "I got in his face and said, 'Hello, James.' Oh, man, did he do a double take."

"He was really surprised?"

"Putting it mildly."

"What'd he say?"

"He said, 'Maribeth? Is that you, Maribeth!' He just kept looking at me like he didn't recognize me. Okay, I've put on weight, but not that much! I can't say the same for him. He hasn't gained an ounce. The bastard looks as good as ever."

"Why was he there? In the diner? Did he know you worked there?"

"How would he know? It's just one of those weird things."

"But what's he doing here?" My hands got cold, and my jaw began to ache. *Did he come back to see me*? The question shot through my mind like a fire.

"He says he's working for a computer company as a roving troubleshooter. This is part of his territory."

"How long is he going to be here?"

"Ha, same thing I asked him, hoping he'd say he was leaving tomorrow." She made a face. "Going to be here a month, six weeks, he has a lot of work at that new plant on Tecumseh Road. Imagine him, a computer expert—how'd that happen? Last time I looked he was using a pick and shovel."

"Really?"

She shrugged. "No, I'm exaggerating. He always had good hands. He could run any machine in the world."

I held my jaw. "Has he been here before?"

"I don't know. All I know is . . . it scared me, seeing him."

"I'm not scared of anything," I said. I don't know why I said it.

"Yeah, well, I'm not as brave as you, I guess." Her face got blotchy. "Seeing him sitting there—it was awful. I wanted to kill him. It scared me to death."

"What are you so scared of? Think I'm going to run off with him?"

She rubbed her eyes, which were dark, tired. "Are you?"

"Not this time."

She leaned farther into the room, as if she were going to fall in. "Don't say that. Don't be flip with me on this subject."

I got up and shut off my desk lamp. "It's all right, Ma," I said. "Don't worry. I'm not going anywhere."

TWENTY-EIGHT

Twenty Questions

Why didn't James Wells ask about me?
Does he remember me?
Is he going to come to our house?
Does he want to see me?
Will he go to the diner again?
Will he ask my mother about me this time?
Should I go there in case he shows up?
Where's he staying?
How long is he going to be around here?
What if I meet him somewhere?
Will I recognize him?
Will he recognize me?
What if he doesn't believe who I am?
Should I carry his picture with me to prove it?
What will I say to him?
Should I just start talking?
What should I call him?

What will I tell him about myself?
What would he want to know?
Would he want to know anything?

❋

TWENTY-NINE

The Phone Number

On the bureau, like artifacts, I laid out the photo of James Wells, the brass buckle, and a slip of paper with a phone number. I rearranged them, so the photo was in the middle. And then again: photo facedown, buckle on top of photo, paper with phone number on top of that. It was James Wells's phone number.

I had gotten it from Dennis. I'd called to ask if he knew that James Wells was in the city. He said yes, Jimmy had called to say hello to him, and he was staying in a motel on Erie Boulevard. "I have the phone number if you want it."

I did. But then I just left it there, on my bureau. I think I was still hoping for something.

One morning, after my mother was gone and before I went to school, I called the number. He answered right away. "Hello. Wells here."

I was sitting on the stairs, with the phone in my lap. I didn't speak. I couldn't. I sat there, transfixed.

"Hello?" He had a quick, deep voice. "Is this Mercer? Hey, guy! I'm not in the mood for games this morning."

I opened my mouth to say something—I had no idea

what—and then I hung up. "Oh god, oh god," I mumbled.

"What's the matter?" Aunt Zis said. She came down the stairs, holding an armful of laundry.

"Nothing." I went into the bathroom and washed my face. *I should have had a tape recorder. I could have gotten his voice. Another artifact.*

I kept splashing my face with cold water.

There was one other thing I had to do that day. I talked to Meadow. "What's the story?" I said in her ear, while the gym teacher tried to get us all to march in a line out of the gym to the playing field. "Still hate me? Still ready to throw our friendship down the drain?"

She stamped her feet up and down. Left, right, left, right . . . "I'm not the one who did it, Jessie."

"You're right, you're right, it's me. Okay, what do you want me to do? Want me to give Jack up? Is that what you want?"

"Oh, you don't like him anymore?"

"No, I do. I like him a lot. But I love you," I said furiously to her back. Why did I have to choose? I didn't want to give him up. I didn't even know if I had the guts to do it. But . . . Meadow was like family. I loved her that way. I couldn't walk out on her, I couldn't just turn my back on her.

We marched past the teacher, who was holding the door open. "Backs straight, people, backs straight," he chanted.

Meadow pushed her hair behind her ears. "Wait a second—do you really want to give him up?"

"No!"

"Then why did you ask me that?" She sounded mad again.

I took in a deep breath. "Because I would."

"For me?"

Was I crazy? "Yes. I would do it for you."

126

There was silence for a moment, then she reached behind her for my hand. "I'll see you in the cafeteria," she said. "Okay? Our usual table."

"She fell asleep on the couch?" my mother said.

I nodded, glancing over at Aunt Zis. "She was watching TV."

"I should get her up to her own bed. What are you doing up so late, anyway?" She straightened the afghan I'd thrown over Aunt Zis, then sat down across from me at the table. "I'm dying for a cup of tea."

"I'll make it. Lemon?"

"And lots of it."

I brought her the tea and glanced at my watch. "I called James Wells," I said. "Dennis gave me his number."

"You talked to him? What was that like?"

"I just called. I listened to his voice. And then I hung up."

"You did what?" She laughed.

"Wait. Don't say anything else." I showed her my watch. "In ten seconds, I'll be fifteen years old."

She put down her cup. "I forgot. I can't believe it."

"Seven . . . six . . . five . . ." I let my hand fall slowly, like the balloon on New Year's. "Four . . . three . . . two . . . one. . . . *Boom.* I'm officially fifteen."

"Congratulations. What do you want for your birthday? Give me a hint. I'll get you something nice."

"Not clothes or anything. Nothing, really." Why even say it? I wanted Aunt Zis to be smart and strong again. I wanted to know what was going to happen to me. I wanted to know the same thing I'd always wanted to know—why James Wells had left me.

"Make a wish," she said. "If you could have one great thing, what would it be?"

"You going to get it for me?"

"Depends how much it costs."

127

"Oh, it can't be that great, right?" I needled. "What I want is free. I wish to see into the future."

"*Easy.*" She tapped my shoulder. "I predict that part of everything you want to happen will happen," she droned. "Part of everything you don't want to happen will happen. Everything you never thought about happening will happen. Nothing will ever stop happening. It will just go on happening all the time."

"Did you read that someplace?"

"No. It's my own crystal ball. It's just life, Jessie, it's like the weather, you get something of everything." She noisily drained the last drops of tea. "Why can't I make good tea like this?"

"You leave the tea bag in too long."

"I know. I put it in, and then I walk away and forget to take it out. . . . So you're fifteen? Come here." She patted her lap.

"Are you kidding? No, thanks!"

"Come on," she said. "We'll be friendly and snuggle a little, the way we used to. You've only been fifteen for five minutes." She reached toward me, hands out, as if she were going to pull me across the table.

"Maybe another time," I said.

But then I got up and plunked myself into her lap. It was ridiculous. I was nearly as big as she was. I sniffed her skin, her hair. She wrapped her arms around me, and I leaned back against her. I let myself be held.

THIRTY

✾

Raspberry Ice Cream

"Look over there," my mother said. We were in the supermarket. "It's him." She pointed to the end of the aisle. Just her index finger moved.

He was wearing jeans and a leather jacket. Sleeked-back hair, dark hair like mine, ending in a thin, small ponytail.

He pushed his cart around the corner of the aisle. I walked after him. "Jessie," my mother said. "Jessie—" Her voice was like a bungee cord; it pulled me, released me, pulled and released.

I saw him leaning over the freezer section. I went and stood next to him. "Hello," I said.

He looked at me. "Hello."

"There's the raspberry," I said, pointing.

"How'd you know that was my favorite?"

"I know quite a few things about you," I said. "For starters, I know who you are, James Wells."

He threw me a startled glance, then a deep guilty flush spread across—

No, it didn't happen like that.

I didn't say anything when I stood next to him at the freezer. I just watched him.

129

He did take a pint of raspberry ice cream, though. He threw it into the cart. Then he took a big white handkerchief from his pocket and wiped his hands, wiped each finger, before putting the handkerchief back.

I'd never imagined him as the sort of person who would wipe his fingers so carefully. I wanted to ask him about it, and I might have. At the moment, it seemed to make as much sense as asking him if he recognized me. As much sense as anything.

Maybe I didn't say anything because there were so many things I could have said and I didn't know which to choose.

I'm Jessie Wells. Remember me? ...

Hello, James, this is Jessie Wells, your daughter, standing in front of you. ...

Do you have any idea, James, how much I've thought about you? Do you have any idea how I've hated you and loved you and wanted to see you and hoped I never would, and cared, and didn't care? ...

So, listen, just tell me this—do you think of me as your daughter? I think of myself as your daughter, but am I, really, if you don't know me?

He pushed the cart toward the front of the store.

I followed him and stood in line behind him. *Tell me where you've been, tell me why you left me, tell me why you've stayed away from me, tell me why it never mattered to you that I was here. ... Tell me. Tell me. Tell me. ...*

He picked up a magazine. He saw me and smiled briefly. It was the smile you give to a stranger. It was the smile a man gives a girl. Kind, meaningless, empty.

✴

THIRTY-ONE

Jumping for the Sun

I'm not quite sure how it happened that Jack and I
found ourselves at the motel where James Wells was
staying on Erie Boulevard. I mean, I know the sequence
of events. But that doesn't completely explain it. The
first thing was that Jack had to buy a shirt and he asked
me if I would come along and help him choose.

"Sure," I said. "As long as I don't have to pay for
it." I could say almost anything to him and make him
laugh.

So we met at the mall, and we did that, we found a
really nice shirt. Blue. He looked great in it. Then it
wasn't very late yet, I still had time before I had to catch
the bus, so we went outside and walked around. And I
looked across the boulevard and noticed the sign for the
motel blinking on and off down the road.

This is where it's a little murky to me. I'm not sure
if I told Jack, and he said, "Why don't we go over
there?" Or if I said, "Let's walk over on the other side."

Whichever, there we were. It was a kind of rambly,
sleazy-looking place, shoved in between a carpet cleaning business on one side and a gas station on the other.
We walked around to the back, to the parking lot, which

faced on a residential street, and then one of those things happened that you think can't possibly happen in real life. The door to one of the rooms opened, and James Wells came out.

He had a couple of bags over his shoulders and he was carrying several heavy square black cases. "That's him," I said. My head started burning. My eyes blurred and his features were blurred. Was it really him?

"That's my father," I said.

I stared at him with the same stupefied feeling I'd had when I phoned him and that I'd had again in the supermarket. I had gone right up to him, followed him like a dog with its nose to the ground. And then I hadn't said a word.

"You going to talk to him?" Jack asked.

"I don't know."

"I will, if you want."

"What?"

"Break the ice for you."

"No . . . okay."

I couldn't think. But while I stood there, half-frozen, Jack walked over and said, as easily as if it was nothing, "Hi, need some help?"

"No," my father said.

"Sure?" Jack said, in his nice way. "I don't mind."

"Okay. Open the trunk." He handed Jack keys and pointed to a green car. Honda, like ours, only a lot newer.

I watched my father load the bags into the car, and I thought, *Tight guy, he's suspicious when help is offered, and he won't say thanks.*

Jack looked over at me and nodded as if to say, *Come on, come on over here.* It dawned on me that my father was leaving, and I might never see him again. *Golden opportunity, Jessie.* Those words came into my mind, but they seemed far away, weak, fragile. *Birds in my stomach beating their wings, wings in my head . . .*

132

Jack said something to my father that drew a smile. It was the first time I'd really seen him smile. I saw the boy in the picture. The boy before he became the man who was my father. My heart beat hard, I almost resented that smile. I didn't want him to be charming, I didn't want Jack to come back to me and say what a nice guy he was.

While I was thinking this, I was also thinking that I should go forward and say something to him. I should say hello, at least. I should get him to talk to me. But I still stood there and thought the same thoughts I'd had so many times before. *Why did you do it? Why did you leave me? You're my father, why didn't you love me enough to stay?*

Suddenly he looked over at me, and we looked straight at each other. He looked right into my face. He knew me. That's what I think. I don't know if it's true, it's just what I feel.

Then he moved his shoulders, like straightening his jacket or shrugging off something. He got into the car and closed the door. Jack stepped back. The engine turned over, and I calmly walked forward. I don't know what was in my mind. My jaw was aching. Later I thought I should have yelled, I should have used my big voice to stop him from driving away.

Jack and I walked back the way we'd come. We waited to cross the boulevard at the light. I looked down at my feet and then up at the sun, and then down at my feet again. Now I'll never know, I thought, I'll never know why he did it.

But maybe there are some things you can never know. Some things you can never understand. Some questions that can never be answered. And some things that will never be.

Maybe wanting something isn't enough. But still, you can try. It's like jumping for the sun. You know you won't make it, but why not jump as high as you can?

133

❁

THIRTY-TWO

Blue Lake

On the way upstairs to call Jack, I stopped and looked back down into the living room. The food was just about destroyed, which meant it must have been good. When we had laid everything out on the table, serve-yourself style, Aunt Zis had said it looked like something that should be in a magazine.

Ma and I had made three different salads, including fruit salad, and Aunt Zis had made a tray of baked chicken with her special orange-juice sauce. Aaron brought a pan of lasagna, bags of chips, and fresh Italian bread. Plus, we had the cake Randy had made at the diner. It was magnificent, it looked like a wedding cake. My mother had asked him to bake it, then she felt guilty and invited him to the party.

"In that case—," I said, and I invited Meadow and Diane. So what started out to be a family party for Aunt Zis's birthday—the three of us, plus Aaron—grew into a bash, including Aunt Zis's senior tap group, our neighbors on both sides, and even Brenda, my mother's favorite of her three bosses.

I toyed with the idea of inviting Jack, but I didn't, because of Meadow. He was still a slightly sore subject between us, although Meadow swore up and down that she was over her crush and never gave him so much as a passing thought anymore.

My mother had put some awful syrupy music on the phonograph, but nobody seemed to mind. She was standing by the window talking to Randy and a couple of our neighbors. Diane was dancing with old Mr. Haviski, from Aunt Zis's tap group, and her brother, Charlie, was off in a corner talking to Meadow. Now that was interesting. Meadow's face was flushed, although from Charlie's body language, it looked like they were only discussing guitars. He had his arms extended and was strumming the air. In the middle of everything, Aunt Zis sat with her back very straight, like a little queen presiding over her subjects. Aaron was on one side of her and Victor Perl had drawn up a chair on the other side.

I'd been torn between wanting to keep his appearance at the party a surprise for Aunt Zis and worry that, if I didn't say anything, she'd insult him by not remembering who he was. He certainly remembered her. "Well, how is she? How is your wonderful aunt?" he'd said when I called to invite him to the party. "Of course I'll come."

I took the phone in my room to call Jack. "Did your aunt get a lot of presents?" he asked.

"She cleaned up! We told everybody no presents, but they brought things anyway. She got cologne, hand lotion, an embroidered glasses case from Diane, an African violet from Meadow, and tons of other things."

"I'm going to have you organize my next birthday party," Jack said. "Don't forget to save me a piece of cake."

"Would I forget that?"

"Would you?"

"I might," I said, "knowing me. Glad you reminded me."

He laughed.

*   *   *

"I have to tell you something," my mother said the next day. We were walking a trail in the state park around Blue Lake. Aaron and Aunt Zis had fallen behind, and we stopped and waited for them.

My mother sat down on a stump. "Remember when we talked about James Wells coming back that time when you were five years old?"

"I remember."

"Well, you know, I thought of something," she went on. "He didn't just drive away that day."

"But that's what you said he did!"

"Well, yes, but then he came back. He was halfway down the street, and then he stopped and backed up, and just as he pulled up again in front of the house, you appeared. You'd come up the side stairs from the backyard, and he saw you. I'm sure that's why he came back—to try to see you. And there you were. Just what I didn't want! I went flying over to you. He stuck his head out the window and yelled, *'She's beautiful.'* "

"He said that?" Way across the lake, a couple was paddling a canoe. I could hear the faint slip of the paddles in the water.

"Yes," my mother said. "He did."

"Why didn't you tell me that before?"

"I forgot. The other day I was thinking about it, and it all came back to me."

I wondered if it was true. I knelt down on the shore and dabbled a stick in the water. I decided that I would take it as true. I would take it as the birthday gift she hadn't given me yet.

The two people in the canoe seemed to be a man and a girl. A father and daughter? They paddled around the bend and out of sight.

Sometimes the phone rings and nobody's there. Silence only. And then I think, It's him. James. My father.

Sometimes I don't think of him for days. The thought of him will come when I least expect it. When I'm on my way to school, or going into the drugstore, or setting the table. Suddenly, there he is, passing through my mind, quickly, like a stiff breeze, a hard wind, something sharp and cool. Here and then gone. Sometimes I want to hold on to the thought of him, but I can never make the moment last any longer than it's going to last.

The next time I see him, if there is a next time, and somehow I think there will be, I know I'm going to speak to him. I'll be ready. And if he can answer my questions, good. And if he can't, well, that'll be okay, too.

But first, before I say anything else, I'll stand in front of him and look into his face and tell him my name. Jessie Wells. I'll say, "I just want you to know I'm related to you. I just want you to know this is who I am, and this is how I turned out."